One

Glasgow, June 1988

A Portrait Group

I'M STARING INTO SPACE, Julie thought. It's my twenty-fourth birthday; I'm single; I have a job; I'm sitting at a desk and staring into space. The problem was the music. Andrew, who was her employer and who ran the gallery, liked to have music playing in the background, whatever was happening. It was not obtrusive – he always kept the volume low – but when, as now, she stopped to think about it, it distracted her from whatever she was doing. Andrew said the clients appreciated it; he said there were studies that showed that people felt more comfortable spending money if there was music in the background. Julie had been doubtful.

"What studies?" she asked. People were always invoking the support of studies, many of which, she was convinced, were apocryphal.

He grinned. "Don't you believe me?"

"I'm not saying that I don't believe you, it's just that there seem to be studies for everything. There are studies that say eggs are bad for you, and then there are studies that say we should eat at least one egg a day."

"That's for the iron," he said. "You need to keep up your iron levels, Julie."

She persisted. "But these music studies?"

He waved a hand airily. "I read about them. They exist. Apparently, music makes you feel less anxious, and if you're less anxious, you're more inclined to spend money."

She sighed. "Even if you know you shouldn't?"

He became serious. "Julie, we're a business – remember. We sell paintings. That's why we're here. Paintings are often a real impulse purchase. That's just the way it is."

She said that she understood. She told him that she did not mind the music too much. It was always discreet. She had no argument with his taste, which was light classical. But on days when Andrew did not come into the gallery – when he was at an auction, or visiting his girlfriend in Edinburgh – she was tempted to turn off the music. It was only her innate honesty that stopped her from opting for silence.

That day she was on her own. Andrew, who was conducting an affair with a woman ten years his senior, had gone off to Edinburgh to meet his lover for lunch, leaving Julie in sole charge of the gallery. She was undaunted by this, even if she found that days spent by herself in the gallery tended to drag, especially when it came to late afternoon. On this occasion, there were a couple of appointments that would break up the day and give her something to do, other than prepare copy for future catalogues.

The first appointment was with an artist. These were meetings that Andrew was keen to delegate to her – at least in the first instance. "You can be the gatekeeper, Julie," he said. "If you find anything remotely interesting in their work, then I'll see them. But in most cases . . ." He sighed. There were too many would-be artists who were convinced that they had talent but who in reality had none – or none that

The Private Side of Friendship

ALEXANDER McCALL SMITH

The Private Side of Friendship

Polygon

First published in hardback in Great Britain in 2025
by Polygon, an imprint of Birlinn Ltd

Birlinn Ltd
West Newington House
10 Newington Road
Edinburgh
EH9 1QS

9 8 7 6 5 4 3 2 1

www.polygonbooks.co.uk

ISBN 978 1 84697 729 9
eBook ISBN 978 1 78885 797 0

British Library Cataloguing-in-Publication Data
A catalogue record for this book is available on
request from the British Library.

Typeset in Adobe Caslon Pro by The Foundry, Edinburgh
Printed and bound in Great Britain by Clays Ltd, Elcograf S.p.A.

This book is for Cheri Bird.

would interest the public, let alone persuade them to make an impulse buy. And it was getting worse, he said. The art schools had signalled their unwillingness to teach traditional drawing and painting skills, and the results were only too evident. "Conceptual art is all very well," Andrew had said to her. "But it's bad news for galleries. You can't hang a concept on a wall."

They had worked out a system. Julie would respond to the artists' first approach. She would ask them to submit photographs of their work. If she thought they were worth a closer look, she would invite them to bring a portfolio to the gallery. If she liked what she saw, she would arrange for the artist to meet Andrew. In most cases, that led to a serious conversation about a future show. It was slow, painfully so at times, and she felt sorry for the artists.

She looked at the diary. *Ralph Macauley. Glasgow School of Art. 11 a.m.*

And now he was there, appearing on the other side of the gallery's glass front door, a young man of about her age, possibly a year or two older. He was neatly dressed – for an artist – and she noted his corduroy trousers, which lent an old-fashioned look to his appearance. That boded well for his ability to paint. Painting was an old-fashioned skill – especially figurative painting of the sort she had seen in the photographs he had sent.

He entered hesitantly. "Am I early?" he asked. There was a note of anxiety in his tone.

She made an effort to put him at his ease. "You're exactly on time."

"I'm Ralph," he said, offering his hand.

They shook hands, and she invited him to sit down.

"I've brought my portfolio." He gestured to the flat black

case he had with him. "And photographs of other works."

She smiled encouragingly. "I'm looking forward to seeing them."

He looked at her as if he was trying to work out whether she meant it. He had shown his work to more than twelve galleries, and none had bitten. Now, he opened the portfolio and took out a few sheets of watercolours and a handful of photographs. He passed these over the desk.

She looked at the watercolours. She nodded. "These are nice."

"Nice?"

He was right to remark on the overused word, she thought and tried to correct herself.

"I mean good. These are good."

She picked up one of the photographs. Her gaze moved away and then returned. It dwelt on the picture.

"And this one," she said, "is lovely."

He caught his breath. "You think so?"

She nodded. "Look at it. Look at the faces . . . Well, you did, didn't you? I take it you know James Cowie's *A Portrait Group*."

He hesitated. "This is different."

She was quick to reassure him that she was not accusing him of plagiarism. "I'm not saying this is based on that. It's just that looking at this picture, your picture, makes me think of Cowie. That painting of his in the National Gallery in Edinburgh. The four young people."

He was still suspicious. "I know it. But I didn't—"

"No, I wasn't saying that. It's just . . . just reminiscent of Cowie . . . that haunting painting of his."

He relaxed. "I agree. Haunting's the right word."

"Haunting, yes." She gestured to the photograph. "As is yours."

He looked pleased. "I knew them," he said.

"The subjects?"

"Yes." He pointed to the young woman on the left of the group of figures sitting round a kitchen table. "Her. She was Maggie. She was one of my flatmates. As were the other three. We shared a flat for three years. The same place. The same people. We were all at the Art College together – in the same year. Two of us shared a birthday."

She looked up. "It's my birthday today."

He smiled. "Congratulations."

She stared at the picture in silence. "It's like one of those interiors by Vuillard," she said. "You know, the ones with pots and pans in the background."

He agreed. "I love those. *Intimisme*. Yes, I suppose it is a bit like that." And then he added, "How can one not like Vuillard?"

He said this with the air of one establishing a shared passion. Of course, there would be nobody to whom Vuillard did not appeal.

She said that she could not conceive of how anyone might be indifferent to Vuillard. "But it's not the background that interests me here," she said. "It's what's going on between the people."

He looked at her with sudden interest. "That's what you see?"

She said that it was. "What I see here is four people on the cusp of something. Four people beginning."

He was staring at her. Had nobody said anything like this to him about this picture? It was the obvious way of looking at it.

She asked whether she was on the right lines.

"Of course you are," he replied. "But it's also about four people saying goodbye to one another. There's that, too."

She was quick to agree. Looking at the picture more closely, she said, "Two of them are looking out – at the artist, so to speak. One is looking over to the left, and the fourth is—"

"Looking at one of the sitters," he supplied.

"Yes."

"Because he was in love with her," he said.

She stared at the grouping of the sitters. "Did she know that?" she asked.

He shook his head. "I don't think so. I may be wrong, but I don't think so."

She asked him whether the young man in the picture had told him about how he felt.

"He didn't have to. I could tell." He paused. "It's hard being in love with somebody who doesn't return your feelings."

"Unreciprocated love."

"Yes," he said. "Unreciprocated. It's common enough, I think."

She studied the photograph again. "It's such an important time in anybody's life, isn't it? You're at an age when you're ready to fall in love. You're at a stage when you make intense friendships very readily. And then suddenly it's all over, and you're by yourself again."

He fixed her with an intense look. "Did you share a flat? Did you go through all that?"

She put the photograph down on her desk. "I did," she said. "I had flatmates. And one of them is getting married in Edinburgh next week. I'll be seeing most of them again. We're all getting together once more."

"You're looking forward to that?"

She hesitated. She was, she decided. Of course, she was looking forward to seeing them again. But it had still made her cry – just the thought of it. It was ridiculous: the prospect of their reunion had made her cry.

She remembered a poem she had read some years before. It was about memory. Memory was an onion – it made you cry. It could make her cry, even after four years. And presumably it would do the same after forty.

She said, "It was four years ago. It was a very difficult time."

"All times are difficult," he said. "In their way."

"And sad."

He reached for the photograph that she had laid back on the table. "I wish I could go back to that time. To that kitchen. With those particular people."

"You can't," she said.

"I know that. But don't you wish the same thing yourself?"

She admitted that she did. "But we're told that we shouldn't be nostalgic. That nostalgia's a bad thing. That we should live in the present rather than the past."

He said, "We're told all sorts of things all the time. There's nothing wrong with nostalgia. You could argue that nostalgia gives you a stronger sense of who you are. And if you have that, your immune system will be healthier and you're less likely to die."

She responded, "We're all bound to die. It goes with human territory."

He was looking at the photograph wistfully. "I was probably happier then than I've ever been. Or will be, I suppose."

She did not say anything. But she thought that what he had

said was true for her too. But now she needed to look at the rest of his portfolio.

"Let's look," she said. "We can talk about the past some other time."

"Of course," he said. "Because one thing about the past – it doesn't go away, does it?"

She closed her eyes for a moment. He was right. The past might fade, might become less vivid, less present, but it did not go away.

Two

Edinburgh, March 1984

No lease for Caravaggio

THERE WAS THAT SMELL. It was, she thought, the characteristic smell of stone – although most people assumed that stone had no smell. But it did, and it was here now, emanating from the flagstones beneath her feet, and from the walls perhaps, although they were for the most part plastered and painted. Plaster had a particular smell too, as did paint – but this stone smell was neither of those.

At the far end of the entrance, spiralling upwards in a tight curve, was the flight of stairs that served the flats that made up the tenement block. The steps, too, were stone, worn away in the middle after all those years of feet going up and down each day, through summers and winters, through two world wars and the fall of empires, local and distant.

That smell – she would have recognised it anywhere – even out of context, because she had always had a good memory for scents. As a child, she would close her eyes and say *vanilla*, or *dates*, or *Patum Peperium, the fish paste that Daddy puts on his toast and that makes me want to throw up*; she could identify these things just by sniffing. Her younger sister, Prue, who throughout her childhood was envious of so much, challenged her, "You think that you can tell anything by its smell – well,

9

you can't. What am I holding in my hand then, if you're so clever?"

She opened her eyes to look at the clenched fist, and then said, "A nutmeg."

Prue tightened her lips. Then came the accusation: "You saw, didn't you? You looked."

"I didn't. You're just cross because I can do things you can't."

Of course, there was the air. Sometimes air could just smell of itself. She was not sure how this worked, but that was how it seemed. Air trapped in a space had a smell that had nothing to do with the things around it. When it was stale, it was as if the air itself had gone off. Perhaps that was why these Edinburgh stairways had that smell. The front door was usually kept closed – those doors were sprung on wheezy closing mechanisms – and there were no open windows. In those conditions, was it surprising that air should smell?

Of course, the dust made a contribution. That smell, that slightly *starchy* smell, was not only stone, but dust as well. People brought dust in with them on their shoes and it could lie there for days until somebody swept it up and washed the steps down with buckets of lukewarm water and mild disinfectant. Perhaps the smell was partly that of the disinfectant – that odour so reminiscent of hospital corridors and small emergencies.

She stood at the foot of the stair and looked up to the glass cupola four floors above her. The morning sun was at just the right angle for the light to fall across the highest of the landings, which was where she was heading. She craned her neck and saw the door on the landing – the door that would be hers if Mrs Donald approved of her, as she hoped she would. She was used to waiting for approval; everything in her life so far, it seemed, had depended on the say-so of others. They said that this changed – that at a certain point in life we all suddenly find ourselves in a position where we no longer depend on the decisions of people in authority – of parents, teachers, employers. They said that you realised you were at that stage when you looked over your shoulder and saw that there was nobody there: that it was you yourself who would give the nod of approval. They said it was like having a window opened on a view that you had only imagined before.

That had not happened to her yet. She was twenty, which was meant to be a significant milestone, but she still felt that her life was not yet her own. She lived independently – but it was still under a roof that belonged to somebody else. She could choose what books she read, but she still had a reading list that other people, the lecturers on her university course, had compiled for her – in those days, the fallacy that we ourselves could decide what we needed to learn had yet to become dogma. And her share of the rent of this flat – if she managed to secure the lease – would be paid by her parents. What would *real* independence be like? What would it be like to wake up one morning and say to oneself: *I can do whatever I like today*?

She started to climb the stairs and, through a habit that had persisted from childhood, she counted them as she made her way up to the top floor. It was a burdensome task, but she continued to do it, as one persists with a ritual that has long since lost its rationale. At the back of her mind was that kernel of superstitious behaviour: the thought that if she failed to perform the necessary ritual, then an unspecified disaster would ensue. It was like the childhood belief that if you stepped on the lines in the pavement, bears would materialise from nowhere and snatch you. She knew where that came from, of course: it was in a half-remembered children's book, in which a small boy in his floppy sunhat went to such pains to avoid standing on the cracks. Childhood's shadow could be a long one.

A friend who was studying psychology, and who, full of new knowledge and a whole fresh vocabulary, had pronounced, "Superstition, Julie. Simple superstition. You count steps – other people don't walk under ladders, or take a seat in the thirteenth row, or they throw salt over their shoulder. It's all the same. It's because we're frightened. We look out on the world and realise we can't control the things that happen to us, and so we invent ways of keeping it all at bay. You count stairs. That's the way it is."

"I could easily give up," she had said. "I really could. I know nothing's going to happen to me."

The friend laughed. "That's the one thing none of us knows. None of us knows what's going to happen to us. We just don't."

One hundred and sixty. A nice, round number, and round numbers were a good sign ...

There were two flats on the landing. On the door of one of them was a small brass plate that read *Edwards*. On the other, a slightly smaller plate, dulled by age and lack of cleaning: *Jas Murray*. She stared at it. It might have read *The late Jas Murray*. *Jas* was the old-fashioned abbreviation for James. Now, in 1984, it had a contemporary ring to it. *Jas* sounded like *Jos* or *Josh*, but struck an androgynous note, which was quite fashionable. *Jas* could be a bass guitarist in a rock group; *Jas*, as in James, had more prosaic possibilities. *Jas Murray* could be a cost accountant or a minor functionary, a man whose life led narrowly and correctly to the grave. He could have been here a long time ago, a century perhaps. She had been told the flat she would be looking for had *Jas Murray* on the door.

She rang the bell. Somewhere within the flat, she heard a buzzer sound. She looked up as she waited. The cupola showed signs of leakage at one corner, where the plaster below it was discoloured. Cupolas leaked. There were cupolas that were weathertight, but they were somewhere else altogether – they were not in Scotland.

The woman who answered the door was somewhere in her sixties, tall and with that well-read look of a certain sort of Edinburgh woman – reticent, perhaps, but with the look of one who had *lived*. She was wearing an Indian print dress, the light cotton fabric faded, as if the sun, somewhere, had bleached it. Julie's eye went to the double gold bracelet – an expensive and unexpected addition tacked on to the modest outfit. She smelled of eau-de-cologne, *4711* – four, seven, eleven, named after the address where it was first produced. She thought: citrus and fruit; not quite lime, nor orange either. A *thin* scent, she thought. Watery. Her grandmother had worn it, dabbed behind her ears and on her wrists, where it had rubbed off on the things she touched. Her grandfather smelled of it from time to time, too. She had brought silence to the family dining room when, at the age of eight, she had announced, "Grandad smells of four, seven, eleven because he has been hugging Granny."

He had raised his eyebrows, and smiled – as he did when she said anything. And then he had said, "Absolutely right. Amazing," and the conversation had resumed.

"You're Julie."

It was more of a statement than a question, accompanying a

quick, and undisguised, look of appraisal.

"I wasn't expecting you just yet."

Julie glanced at her watch apologetically. She had been careful to be on time.

"I'm sorry. I thought—"

The woman interrupted her. "No, my fault. I was reading something, and lost track of time. I hadn't realised it was so late." She smiled again, and gestured for Julie to come in.

The flat was spacious, as were many Victorian flats in that part of Edinburgh. They were in a hall from which one door led to a corridor, while others gave onto surrounding rooms. Two were open, allowing light to flood in from the rooms beyond. Being on the top floor, a skylight added to the brightness.

"I'm Lisa Donald," said the woman. "I should have introduced myself properly. We spoke on the phone, of course."

She led them through to a sitting room at the front of the flat – a large room dominated by a fireplace with a carved wooden mantelpiece. The furniture was comfortable – two sofas, one of which was covered with a tartan throw; several easy chairs; a writing table; a capacious bookcase now largely denuded of books. There were several framed pictures: a seascape, a print in a style that Julie recognised.

Mrs Donald saw that Julie had noticed the print. "Bawden," she said.

"I know," said Julie. "I love him. Bawden, Ravilious, Nash – I like all of them. But Edward Bawden in particular . . ."

Mrs Donald smiled. "Come and take a closer look."

They stood before the picture. There was a family picnicking under a tree. One of the children was playing with a top. The father smoked a cigarette. The sky was largely empty of clouds.

It was England, and the innocence of England.

"It's the little details," said Mrs Donald. "Look at the father. His hair has a parting. And it's very well trimmed, isn't it? That dates him, I'd say. And he's smoking, naturally."

"Everyone smoked in those days. When was this? Nineteen-fifty something?"

Mrs Donald nodded. "More or less. He also did a lot in the sixties, I think. And yes, people smoked a lot more. Look at films of the time. Actors said they needed something to do with their hands. Smoking solved that one."

"I like what this picture says about stillness," said Julie.

Mrs Donald paused and looked at her with interest. "You're interested in art?"

"It's what I'm studying – history of art."

Mrs Donald looked thoughtful. "They didn't say. They just said 'student'. Perhaps they didn't want to put me off. Artists, you see – parties and so on."

Julie laughed. "That's the real artists – the people at the Art College – painters and so on. They have a more . . . more interesting life than people like me. We sit in libraries and read about Caravaggio and so on." Caravaggio; she liked the name, the sounds of it, and its ring of the exotic.

Mrs Donald raised an eyebrow. "Caravaggio? I'm not sure that I'd want to let a flat to Caravaggio." She paused. "I'd have to put it tactfully, of course. I'd say, 'I'm terribly sorry, Mr Caravaggio, but I've decided to give the flat to another tenant. Nothing personal, you understand.'"

Julie grinned. It was clear that Mrs Donald was not a typical Edinburgh landlord. "You wouldn't want to get on the wrong side of Caravaggio. No, I just mentioned him because we had a lecture about him earlier this morning. I know that his private life was colourful – to put it mildly."

"Perhaps we all have an inner Caravaggio," said Mrs Donald. "Deeply buried, in most cases, but occasionally surfacing perhaps." She smiled. "That would be a good title for a book: *Your Inner Caravaggio*."

"With tips on how to live a dangerous life?"

Mrs Donald nodded. "We shouldn't expect artists to be bourgeois. Art would be very dull if they were."

They moved away from the Bawden print. "As you can see," said Mrs Donald, "this flat has remarkable views. Look at what you see from this window, for instance. There are the Meadows down there . . ."

There were trees on the edge of the expanse of green. The wind moved their foliage.

"And the Infirmary, of course. You see those balconies at the end of the buildings? The patients sat out there for the benefit of sunlight. Doctors used to love sunlight. They treated TB with it."

The distant roofs of the Victorian hospital were topped with architectural *jeux d'esprit*. Spikes. Castellations.

"I was looking at a photograph of a ward in the Infirmary," said Mrs Donald. "It was taken in Edwardian times. The beds were all lined up against the walls symmetrically, the covers ironed into knife-edges. There was a grand piano in the middle of the ward, with a large vase of flowers on it."

"A grand piano?"

"Yes. I assume they entertained the patients with piano recitals." She paused. "And people got better, with all that formality. The nurses' starched uniforms. Matron with her cap and her watch pinned onto her breast upside down. All of that helped."

Julie gazed out of the window. "And you can just see the Castle. Just."

"Yes. Bill, my brother – he used to live here, you see – I didn't. It was his flat. Bill used to sit in this alcove looking out towards the Castle. He said that he found it reassuring. The world could be falling to bits, but the Castle was always there on its rock, through thick and thin. He did the crossword each day in that chair, right up to the day before he died. The *Scotsman* crossword."

"I can't do cryptic crosswords," Julie confessed. "I don't get them."

"Bill said it was a question of practice. He said that once you got used to a compiler's – or, more specifically, a cruciverbalist's – style it was easy. He said the solutions came to mind without any effort. He said that the unconscious mind came up with the words. He told me it was like playing the piano. A pianist doesn't have to think where the fingers go – they go there automatically. It's like walking – we don't have to think about it – we do it. Brain pathways, or something like that."

They left the living room.

"There are five bedrooms," said Mrs Donald. "Six, if you use the dining room too. The bedrooms aren't big, but they'll do. You'll all be students, I take it?"

Julie nodded. "That's what I had in mind. I have a friend I'm hoping to share with. She's a girl on my course. And we'll find others – to help with the rent. There are lots of people looking for a room in a flat – even at this point in the academic year. They don't like university accommodation. Halls are okay, but . . ."

"Of course. All . . . all girls? Or . . ."

The question hung in the air, as Julie hesitated. Then she asked, "Is that a condition?"

Mrs Donald shook her head. "Not at all. You can have boys as well. It's just that I wouldn't want to let to a group of boys by themselves. You know what young men are like. They don't take the same care of things."

Julie relaxed. "I do. I have two older brothers. Their rooms were pigsties. They were public health hazards."

"Not all of them, of course. There are *particular* men." She gave Julie a look that suggested she was wondering how far shared assumptions could be relied upon. Attitudes were changing, or had changed. Somebody had expressed surprise that she should refer to men as boys. But they were. They used the word themselves, and she referred to her friends as *the girls*.

"Of course."

Mrs Donald looked thoughtful. "I don't want to impose too many conditions," she said. "But one thing is very important. I don't want too many people living in the flat. I've heard of student flats where there are far too many tenants. Ten, eleven – it has an effect on the fabric of the place."

Julie said that she understood.

"So," continued Mrs Donald. "Six, and no more. All right? That's really important."

"I promise you," said Julie. "Six people, and no more."

Mrs Donald smiled. "It's good to hear somebody promising something. We don't talk about promises very much these days – probably because people don't take them seriously. In my day, you never broke a promise – never. If you did, you felt terrible. You thought that you'd be struck down by lightning – it was a great disincentive."

Julie laughed. "Don't worry. I promise you – six people."

They went into the kitchen. "There's everything you need here," said Mrs Donald. "Bill was a widower. His wife died of breast cancer. He cooked for himself for years." She paused. "I miss him, you know. I miss him terribly. Sometimes I think I should sell this place because whenever I come round here it brings back memories. But I can't bring myself to do it."

Julie nodded in sympathy. "Brothers can be very special."

"Yours? The untidy ones?"

"I love them to bits," said Julie.

"That's how it should be. We have to love one another, don't we? There's a line in a poem about that. *We must love one another or die.* It's true, don't you think?"

Julie hesitated. Did this woman really want an answer? Do you correct the person you hope will let you a flat? In her final year at school, they had read that poem as a class. Their English teacher had told them that the final line had been changed from *We must love one another* or *die*, to *We must love one another* and *die*. That was quite different, they were told, because it meant that the poem became one about inevitability. Life would be disappointing, whatever we did. Love might make it temporarily easier to bear, but ultimately it changed nothing.

"I think it is," she said eventually. "True."

Mrs Donald looked at her. It was a reprise of the look of appraisal she had given her when she answered the door. "You can have the lease, if you want it," she said.

Julie had not expected this so soon. She had thought there might be others interested.

"Are you sure?"

Mrs Donald laughed. "Of course, I'm sure. They told you

about the rent? That's all right with you?"

"Fine," said Julie.

"In that case, I'll tell the solicitors to draw up the lease for you to sign. When do you want in?"

She did not hesitate. There was nothing about this place that she did not like, and she had had enough of the dingy flat she shared with three other students off the Grassmarket. She could not move in soon enough. "Tomorrow?" she said, smiling at her presumption. "But could we make it a week from now – if that suits you?"

Mrs Donald shrugged. "It's all the same to me. I'll phone the lawyer this afternoon." She paused. "He sings, you know. He has a fine baritone voice. If you go to any of the Gilbert and Sullivan Society productions at the Church Hill Theatre, he's always in the cast. It was *The Mikado* last time. He was Pooh-Bah, the Lord High Everything Else."

Julie smiled, a buffoonish Pooh-Bah on stage would be entertaining; in real life, less so.

"May I ask one thing?" Mrs Donald frowned. "Your name: it's a bit unusual in Scotland. The painter? You aren't by any chance—"

"My grandfather," said Julie. "He was my grandfather."

"I thought as much," said Mrs Donald. "When you mentioned that you were studying history of art, I thought there might be a connection." She paused. "I always admired his work. I know that Peploe and Fergusson got all the attention, but your grandfather was every bit as good as they were – in my opinion."

"That's what we think, too," said Julie.

"I went to that retrospective they had in the National Gallery," Mrs Donald went on. "I thought it showed just what a great painter he was. You saw it, of course?"

"Yes."

"And you liked the book that went with it?"

"Very much."

"The art world can be fickle," Mrs Donald mused. "Reputations wax and wane. Your grandfather's will grow – I'm sure of it."

They made their way into the hall.

"The scent you're wearing," said Julie. "I do like it."

Mrs Donald seemed surprised. "I hope it's not overpowering."

"Four, seven, eleven."

There was another glint of surprise. "You know it?"

"I do."

They stood at the front door, slightly awkwardly now, and Julie wondered whether she had crossed some boundary. But she had not. Mrs Donald reached out to touch Julie's forearm – a discreet gesture of approval, and friendship. "The lawyer will be in touch," she said.

"The baritone?"

Mrs Donald inclined her head. "Yes, Pooh-Bah. And you can pick up the keys from their offices in Rutland Square."

"Thank you."

"I have a feeling you're going to be happy here."

Three

A room somewhere

JULIE COLLECTED THE KEYS from the lawyer's office. He was with another client when she arrived, and she had to wait twenty minutes before she was fetched from the waiting room by an awkward young man with angry skin. The young man said to her, "You're lucky. Mr Forth doesn't like students. He warns his clients against letting to them." He put a hand to his face in an apparent struggle not to scratch. "I shouldn't be telling you this, I suppose."

"But he must have been a student once," she said.

"I guess." The young man grinned. "He thinks he can sing. He made us all go to hear him last night. They're doing Gilbert and Sullivan up at the Church Hill. *The Gondoliers*. It was dire. The whole office went."

He gave her an interested look. She lowered her eyes, ashamed at herself at the distaste she felt for him. If you ignored his skin problem, he was not bad looking. As he led her along a corridor, he tried to walk beside her, but there was not enough room. "You go first," she said.

"Do you like the flat?" he asked. "It's handy for the uni, isn't it?"

She agreed, but said nothing further.

"I did law," he said. "I finished last year. I lived near the Pleasance, which was handy for the Old Quad. Do you know the World's End pub?"

She gave a non-committal answer. "I've seen it."

"We still go there, a group of us."

"Oh, yes?"

"Do you fancy joining us there some time?

"Not really. But thanks, anyway."

She wondered what made him think that he would appeal to her? What would they talk about? His life was this office, with its deedboxes and its smell of old documents. You had to be able to talk to a lover about things that moved you. That, after all, was what made a love affair – the discovery of another person with whom you could talk in the dark. Who said that? She remembered now: it was her friend, Annabel, who had been the first at school to have a proper boyfriend. They had listened to her, open-mouthed in their admiration of what they saw as Annabel's sheer bravery. He was called Richard, and he did not last long, but she had imagined the two of them lying in the dark and talking. Remembering that now, she smiled, but thought, that will come to me one of these days. He was there – somewhere; a confidant, a soul mate; a man who lived for art and could discuss with her the things she wanted to discuss. What was the point of sharing one's life with another person if you could not talk to him about how you felt? She had always wondered how many marriages were like that. Her parents, it seemed, were together by force of not much more than habit. How could you be fulfilled if the person with whom you spent your life was like the country you happened to inhabit – just there – a given in the background?

Her response made him redden, and she realised he must be used to rebuffs. With skin like that, perhaps that was what you experienced. She tried to make amends. "It's kind of you," she said. "But my boyfriend likes going to the Golf Tavern. Do you know it? On the Meadows – the far side."

The Golf Tavern existed, but not the boyfriend. It would make him feel better, though.

They had reached a door. "I've never been there," said the young man. "Anyway, this is it. Mr Forth. I'll tell him you're here."

She was taken in. The office was tidy, and the lawyer's desk was largely clear. He rose to his feet as she went in, nodding curtly to the young man, who withdrew and closed the door behind him. The lawyer invited her to sit down.

"I heard from Mrs Donald that you've viewed the property," he began. "I take it that everything is in order – from your point of view?"

"Yes. Thank you – it's fine. It's a nice flat."

He looked at her over his reading glasses. He had a sheath of papers in his hands. "It certainly is. Those Marchmont flats are spacious, and this one, as I recollect, has a fine view."

She pictured him in *The Gondoliers* – wearing one of those black hats that real gondoliers wear. *We're called gondolieri, But that's a vagary . . .* She liked Gilbert and Sullivan because their tunes and words were so sunny. Perhaps that was why he liked them, too, she thought – their operettas took him away from this office, from the box files, and the young man, and the leases and all their clauses.

The lawyer put the papers down on his desk and adjusted his glasses. "Mrs Donald tells me you're a student."

She wondered whether he might have the final say – whether he could somehow overrule Mrs Donald's approval. She waited.

"Do you mind my asking what you study?"

"It's history of art."

She looked for a reaction. It would have been better, she thought, if she had been able to say geography or accountancy, or something that a lawyer might find more reassuring. Art was about . . . well, it was about things that were not *this*. Although seventeenth-century Dutch artists liked to paint *stuff*, she thought: all those pictures of rooms filled with possessions – porcelain, vases of flowers, lobsters.

His expression did not change. "I see. Art."

"Well, history of art, actually. I can't paint. It's about schools of painting, I suppose. How people reacted to the times. What they were doing with their paintings."

He touched the side of his spectacles, as if he were trying to bring the world back into focus. "Have you ever been to Florence?" he asked.

She had. She had gone with her parents after she finished school. It had been their treat for her on finishing that stage of her education. Her father, though, had suffered from food-poisoning and had spent most of their stay confined to the hotel.

"You'll be familiar with the Uffizi, then?"

"I've been there." She looked pointedly at what she imagined was the lease.

"I very much like the *Rites of Spring*," he said. "You know that painting? It's a Botticelli. I have a soft spot for it."

"I know it."

He looked down at the papers in front of him. "You'll be sharing, Mrs Donald says."

"Yes."

He looked up at her. "With whom? Other students?"

"Yes."

He nodded. "And you already know these people?"

She shook her head. "One of them. I have a friend who's going to help me find others."

He considered this. "One has to be careful about sharing with people one doesn't know. You'll be responsible for any damage, of course. You'll remember that, I hope. That's a term of the lease."

He tapped the papers in front of him.

"I know," she said.

"We've had clients who've had awful trouble with these shared flats," he said. "I can't say that I think it's a very good idea."

She did not think he expected a response.

"You have to be careful about the wrong sort," he continued. "There are some people who are irresponsible. There always are."

"I'll be careful."

He looked up from the papers. "You'll see that the number of people staying in the flat is limited to six. You're aware of that?"

He passed the lease over to her. "You should read through this before you sign. I can answer any questions you may have. There's no hurry."

"I'm sure it's all right."

He frowned. "You should still read it."

She took the papers from him, and began to read. He stood up and walked to the window. He looked out, his back towards her. She heard him singing under his breath: a snatch of song, as if he were unaware of her presence.

"Gondoliers," she muttered.

He turned round, and she saw the look of disbelief on his face.

"There's a production on at the moment," he said. "The Gilbert and Sullivan Society. We're doing *The Gondoliers*. It has three more days to run."

"I hope it's going well."

He hesitated. "Would you like a couple of complimentary tickets?"

There was a note of hopefulness in his voice. Attendance, she thought, might not be all that good. And suddenly she felt sorry for him – and for the young man with the troubled skin. Presumably he had worked through all his friends, cajoling them into supporting the production. Now he was down to her – a more or less complete stranger.

"I'm not sure . . ."

The fact that she did not decline outright appeared to encourage him. "Let me give you the tickets. If you can't use them, you can't use them. But I think you might enjoy our efforts."

She did not demur, and twenty minutes later, after she had finished skimming through the provisions of the lease and had signed it, she left the office with her two tickets and the keys to the flat that was to be her home, she hoped, for the two remaining years of her time at university. She went out into Rutland Square and gazed up at the trees in the garden making up the centre of the square. Some architectural squares, it seemed, were not squares at all, but were rectangles, in the same way as some circles were really ovals. She thought about that for a few moments as she started to make her way to the flat that was, from this moment, now hers. She felt the weight of the responsibility. She was *it* – apart from her friend,

Angela, who was ready to join her in the flat that afternoon, and with whom she would set out to find four other students to share the rent. She had already decided that they would divide the place between the sexes, and she thought Angela would agree to that. There would be three women and three men. Equal. Neither would be able to gang up against the other. And they would get people who pulled their weight. They would get people who kept the place tidy. They would get people who washed the bath out after every use. They might even get people who would become friends.

In the flat that afternoon, looking down from the window of the sitting room, Angela said, "Oh, I never imagined . . ." And then, turning to Julie, who was standing just behind her, went on, "How did you find this? It's . . . it's . . ." She struggled unsuccessfully to find the words to express how she felt.

"Happy?" asked Julie.

"Happy? Yes. Speechless."

"Good."

Angela took a step towards Julie. She reached out and flung her arms around her friend, embracing her in a hug. And she kissed her on the cheek. Julie recoiled slightly, taken by surprise at the sudden intimacy. She was not sure how she felt. She did not particularly like being kissed, but Angela was a friend, and friends kissed one another without it amounting to very much – other than a display of friendship.

"Sorry," said Angela, releasing her. "It's just that when you said you had found a flat, I thought it would be . . . well, dingy. I was thinking of a typical student flat somewhere off Newington Road. You know the sort – something like that. And now you've found this place, with this view, and all this space, and . . ." She looked up at the ceiling. "And a cornice. See that? We're going to live in a flat with a cornice."

Julie followed her gaze to the cornice. She was not sure what was so special about a cornice – ceilings had them, and she had never paid much attention to them. But this one clearly meant something to Angela.

Angela intercepted her gaze. "It's just that I've never had a cornice. I know that sounds odd, but where I come from, you see, we have walls . . ."

Julie laughed. "That's a relief."

"We have walls," Angela continued. "And the walls go up to the ceiling. And that's it. No frills. No artistic flourishes. No cornices."

"So, cornices are middle-class? Is that what you're saying?"

Angela shrugged. "Maybe. Maybe not. All I'm sure about is that I really like this place. And that's down to you. You found it." She paused. "What about the bedrooms? Who's going to go where? You should have the best one, you know. You found this. You choose. And then me, I suppose, and then we can let the others fight it out."

"The others . . . We'll have to do something about them. Seeing as the others don't exist yet. I thought we'd get one more girl and then three boys. Equal numbers are best, don't you think?"

"We could, if that's what you want. As I said, you found this place, and so you have the right to decide."

Julie said that she did not want to make all the decisions by herself. "You signed up. It's me and you, I think. We should choose together."

"If that's what you want," said Angela.

"It is." Julie hesitated. "What if we didn't bother to choose?"

Angela frowned. "What do you mean?"

Julie explained what she had in mind. "If we stick up an ad in the Student Union or wherever, we'll get a whole bunch of people applying. There are always more people than there are flats. We all know that."

"We could interview," Angela suggested. "Just to see that they're okay."

Julie asked how she thought they would do that. "Would we ask them questions about how they see themselves living with us? What are they going to say?"

Angela shrugged. "They'll say what they think we want to hear."

"Precisely," said Julie. "So, do we use our intuition? Do we see what we *feel* about them? And if you reach a decision on how you feel about somebody when you first see them – and only for a few minutes – you're almost certainly going to be wrong. Appearances can be misleading."

Angela made a gesture of resignation. "Should we go for first come, first served? Isn't that making it all a bit too random?"

"Yes, it is random, but I think that sometimes random things work out better than planned things. I just have that feeling. I just do. Chance is sometimes best."

Her first meeting with Angela had been a matter of chance. They had both been in a university coffee bar. It had been crowded, and when, having picked up her order, Julie had started to make her way to a table, her arm had been bumped by young man making his way to the door. He had been apologetic, as was Julie to Angela, who had been standing nearby and whose jeans were spattered by a few drops of coffee.

Angela made little of it. "There are too many people in here," she said. "It's nothing, anyway."

Julie put her cup down on a table and offered Angela a tissue. "Use this."

Angela shook her head. She had also been carrying a mug of coffee, which she now put down on the same table. "It's nothing."

"We might as well sit down," said Julie. "Unless you're meeting somebody."

Angela replied that she was by herself. "I've just been to the most boring lecture of my life," she said. "I need this coffee."

Julie smiled. "There should be an award for that. Soporific lecture of the year."

"There's a guy in my class who goes to sleep," said Angela. "He sleeps in every lecture. Somebody said that he hasn't got anywhere to live, and so he sleeps in lecture halls. Sometimes you see him wake up and start to take notes. Then he drops off again."

Julie asked her what she was studying. She hardly needed to ask the question, she felt; there was a certain look to people doing English degrees. It was difficult to put one's finger on it – but it was there.

"English."

"I thought so," said Julie.

"Oh? Why?"

Julie shrugged. "Will you take offence if I say that people who study English literature have a slightly dreamy look about them? It's as if they're somewhere else." She paused. "That sounds a bit rude – it's not meant to be. It's an imaginative look, I suppose."

She looked at Angela as she spoke. There was a sensitivity

there, she decided. And she was sure it was sensitivity rather than dreaminess. "There are some people I can picture reading Jane Austen," she went on. "And some I can't."

"And you can see me doing that?"

Julie looked at her as if summing her up. "Yes, I think so. Tell me what you're reading at the moment?"

Angela took a few moments to reply. "For enjoyment, or for the course?"

"Both."

"For pleasure, I'm reading *Middlemarch* because I like George Eliot. All eight hundred pages."

"I've read that," said Julie. "I felt so sorry for that woman. What was her name?"

"Dorothea."

"Yes. Marriage was a life sentence in those days." She paused. "And for your course?"

"At the moment, that's *Beowulf*. Everybody has to read *Beowulf* – or try to – if they're doing a degree in English. It's a sort of rite of passage."

"I've never read it," said Julie. "I've heard of it, but that's as far as it goes."

"*Beowulf* and Chaucer. You have to do them. In Edinburgh they throw in some medieval Scottish poets while they're about it. Henryson. I rather like him."

"And Burns?"

Angela said she suspected some of her lecturers thought Burns a bit beneath them. "Anything that's too popular is suspect. Not all of them are like that, but there are a few. One of them made a throwaway comment about Burns the other day. She said that he was painfully sentimental."

"Really? I thought that Burns was . . . sort of sacred."

"Not with her," said Angela. "She's pretty hard-nosed. She's in favour of realism, and she doesn't like his attitude towards women. She says he was a philanderer. She accused him of treating women as objects."

Julie frowned. "I suppose he did write *My Love Is Like a Red, Red Rose*. That's objectifying women, if you like – calling them red, red roses."

Angela laughed. "Maybe. But people still get teary-eyed over Burns – even the feminists. They have a soft spot for him because he actually liked women. Some men who . . . who objectify women, don't like them." She fixed Julie with an enquiring look. "And you? What are you studying?"

"Have a guess."

Angela pursed her lips. "It's not mathematics. Am I right?"

"No, it's not mathematics."

"Mathematicians don't talk to people they meet in coffee bars," said Angela. "They have social issues. Some might say they're socially challenged."

"So?"

"I'll say sociology. Maybe psychology. Something like that. Something to do with people."

It was, thought Julie, a flattering guess. "History of art, actually."

"I was about to say that," said Angela, grinning. "But I thought it too obvious. Most of the people you see around here wearing expensive clothes are studying art history. Listen to them. Botticelli, the Renaissance, Giotto, blah, blah, blah—" She stopped herself. "Sorry, I didn't mean to say all that."

Julie knew what Angela was driving at. There were students from privileged backgrounds who studied art history because it was something that people like them studied. They stood out in various ways, one of which could be their clothes. But she was not like them. Many of them came from the same sort of expensive English schools and were studying in Edinburgh because they could not get into Oxford or Cambridge. For them, Edinburgh was a sort of northern Chelsea. She was not like that.

"I'm not of that crowd, for a start," she said. "I'm Scottish."

"I can tell that," said Angela. "You don't talk through your nose – or look down it. It was rude of me."

"No, it wasn't. You were simply stating the obvious. Those people exist – my course is full of them. But my clothes aren't expensive. A friend gave me this – and she had bought it second-hand. The cloth's lovely."

Angela reached out to touch the russet herringbone tweed. "It's beautiful." Her hand lingered.

"It's beautiful, isn't it?" said Julie.

Angela withdrew her hand. "Lovely. I saw Harris tweed being woven up there, you know. We went to visit an aunt who lives on Lewis. She took us to a neighbour, a crofter, who had one of those old looms, the ones you pedal. He was weaving the cloth on that. It was slow, but that's the whole point. That was probably made by somebody like him, but quite a long time ago."

Julie nodded at the thought, then said, "Where do you live?"

"Now? In Edinburgh? Or do you mean where am I from?"

"Tell me where you're from," said Julie. "You don't mind, do you?"

"Why should I?" replied Angela. "It's nowhere special." She gestured towards a group seated at another table. There was loud, confident laughter. "People like that, you see, would never even have heard of where I'm from. You might, but they won't. It's beneath their notice."

"They aren't necessarily snobs," Julie pointed out. "You may be doing them an injustice."

"Am I?" asked Angela. "Well, maybe. But they still won't have heard where I'm from." She sighed, as if weary at the thought of describing something that was difficult to describe. "It's a small town called Armadale. It's in West Lothian – just outside Edinburgh."

It was, she said, nothing special. It was in a mining area, although the mines in its immediate vicinity had closed once the coal seams were exhausted. There had been few notable events in its history – other than a famous highway robbery in the nineteenth century. The perpetrators had been caught and sentenced to death, but one of them was helped to escape by relatives and ended up in New York. "Some people still talk about it as if it were yesterday," she said. "But then Scotland is a bit like that, don't you find? We talk about the Highland Clearances as if they happened a few years ago, rather than starting in the eighteenth century. And the defeat at Culloden still hurts some people who certainly weren't around in 1745."

"Unpleasant memories last longer than pleasant ones," said Julie.

Angela looked at her. "Are you sure about that?"

Julie said that she was, although Angela's questioning raised a doubt in her mind. People suppressed bad memories and cultivated good ones. It was important to remember that you had been happy, even if you forgot *why* you felt that way.

Angela steered the conversation back to Armadale. "There are plenty of towns like Armadale in Scotland," she said. "A lot of them are places where people simply live – because they happen to live there. These places may have had a reason to exist a long time ago, but that reason has usually disappeared. There were brickworks in Armadale, but Scotland stopped making many of the things we used to make. Nothing lasts for ever."

She did not dislike Armadale – it was her home town, after all. And yet she recognised its limitations. Nothing happened there, she felt: everything you read about, everything that was colourful and exciting in the world, was taking place elsewhere – in London or New York, or even, if you stayed in Scotland, in Edinburgh or Glasgow. To stay in Armadale was to be on the periphery for ever.

"I lived with my parents and my grandmother," Angela went on. "My father used to be a mechanic. He worked not far away, in Bathgate, at the bus garage there. Then he was diagnosed with emphysema. Do you know what that is? It's a lung condition that makes you short of breath. He used to smoke – because just about everybody smoked in those days – and that's one of the main causes. He sometimes uses oxygen. He had to stop work, and so my mother went back to work. She has a job as a dental receptionist. My gran stays at home most of the time. That's us. That's home. Nothing special, you see. Ordinary working class."

At school, she was the one they had ambitions for. Most of her year did not go to university: they took apprenticeships or went to work in Bathgate or Edinburgh. Two of the boys joined the army at sixteen. It was going to be different for Angela.

"The English teacher, Mr Macleod," she told Julie, "wanted me to go to university. He gave me books – gave them, from his own collection. He said that if he could get one of his students, just one, to study English at the University of Edinburgh, then he could retire happy."

She had not required much persuasion. Her appetite for reading grew, and she devoured everything Mr Macleod gave her.

"I saw books as the way out of the place where I had been born and brought up. Books were a sort of door. On the other side of the door was the world that I desperately wanted to be part of. This. Edinburgh. Discussing books. Meeting people from other places." She looked at Julie, wondering whether somebody, who had obviously spent her entire life so far in that other world, would understand what it was to be on the outside looking in. Of course, Julie did, and now she said, "Yes, I can imagine."

"Can you?"

"Yes."

"Although the place *you* come from is very different. You were at school in Edinburgh, weren't you?"

"Is it that obvious?"

"Yes, it is, I'm afraid."

Julie sighed. "Oh well. None of us can help being born where we were born."

"Nor who our parents are," added Angela.

"My father's an accountant," said Julie. "He's in a firm. We're not all that well-off."

"But not poor."

"No, we're not poor." Now Julie glanced at her watch. "I have a tutorial in ten minutes," she said. "I'd better—" She stopped herself. An idea came to her. "Do you live at home?"

"At the moment," said Angela. "It's cheaper. I come into

Edinburgh every day. It doesn't take too long, but I'm getting tired of the bus journey. This year I've got enough to pay rent. My father got some compensation from the bus company, you see. He's given some of it to me. I can use that."

Julie hesitated, but decided to ask. "Are you looking for a room?"

"Not yet. I'm going to start, though."

"I'm going to see somebody about a flat in Marchmont. It's ten minutes from here. Fifteen, maybe. I haven't seen it, yet, but if I get the lease, I'm going to need flatmates." She paused. "I may not get it, of course."

"If you do," said Angela, "I'd like to be one of them. Your flatmates."

"Are you sure? I don't have anybody else in mind. I can't guarantee that they'll be . . . what you'd like."

"I don't care," said Angela. She reached out to take Julie's hand. "Please."

Four

Willow will do

THE ADVERTISEMENT JULIE PINNED on a notice board in the Student Union building was answered within two hours. The female voice on the telephone sounded defeated.

"You haven't let it already, have you? I've only just seen your ad, but I thought it might have been up for ages." She paused. "I've missed four flats."

Julie was reassuring. "No. It's only just gone up. And you're the first person to call."

"It's just that flats go so quickly. You have to know somebody, and even then . . ." She trailed off, as the realisation dawned of what had just been said. "You mean, it's still free?"

"Come and take a look."

She seemed unbelieving – as if she had been the beneficiary of an unexpected and inconceivable favour. "Could I? Really? Today?"

That afternoon, Georgia stood on the opposite side of the road, looking up at the Victorian tenement building. Only one side of the street was terraced – the other was open to the parkland known as the Meadows, and was lined with trees. In the distance, beyond these trees, was the city skyline with its spikes and spires. The sky was clear, and the air had that attenuated bright sparkle of north.

She stood for a few minutes, looking up at the building, trying to work out which would be the windows of the flat. She had been told that it was on the top floor, but there would be more than one flat off the landing and there were eight windows to choose from. The sun glinted off several of them, and she shaded her eyes to get a better view. Whichever flat it was, the position was perfect. Her current flat was in Tarvit Street, a narrow alley behind the King's Theatre, and had no outlook beyond the tenement opposite, with its blackened stone and its shabby doorways. She was sharing it with a medical student, a young woman from Aberdeen who used the flat simply as somewhere to sleep. She led a real life, Georgia thought: a life of ward duties, and anatomy tests; of sessions patching people up, and even seeing people die. She left her medical textbooks open on the kitchen table, and Georgia had to avert her eyes in distaste. "Squeamish?" said her flatmate. "Sorry. We get used to it, I suppose."

Georgia looked up again. This would be different. There was light and there was sky. You would not feel depressed here, as she could do from time to time in Tarvit Street.

She drew in her breath. *I have to have it. I have to.*

She was tall. She had heard a friend describe her as willowy, which she did not mind. If there were to be arboreal metaphors, then willow was preferable to oak – too solid – or a pine, too ordinary. Willow would do.

Her hair was somewhere between brown and blonde, and was worn long, held back from her face to reveal high cheekbones. As another friend once remarked, she looked as if she was about to go off and play a game of hockey. It was a healthy look.

Nominal determinism: it seemed so natural to at least some

who knew her that she was called Georgia. It was a name that had a certain ring to it – an air of confidence, of capability perhaps. Georgia was not an uncertain name, which came, in part perhaps, from the fact that the stress fell on the first syllable. There was something determined in the way a first syllable might proclaim itself.

From their window on the top floor, Julie and Angela looked down on the street below. They had seen her arrive and gaze up at the building, shielding her eyes from the sun.

"You said she's called Georgia?" asked Angela, squinting to get a better view.

"Yes."

Angela nodded, as if a revealing detail had been confirmed. "That's her then. She's a Georgia. Tall. Sure of herself. Look at the way she's standing."

Julie smiled. "Can you tell?"

"Of course. People almost always fit their names. Or grow into them."

Julie asked how you could grow into a name.

"It's because of other people," replied Angela. "They treat you in a particular way because they've decided what you are like. And they reach that conclusion on the basis of your name."

Julie looked doubtful. "Prejudice?"

"You could put it that way. And then – and this is the important thing, apparently – you act accordingly. People expect you to be something – and you respond."

"I don't know about that," said Julie.

"If you're a boy and you're called Cecil," said Angela. "People think you're going to be . . . well, I suppose, a bit fussy. So, you act like that because we act as we think people want us to act.

I know it sounds odd, but that's what we do."

Julie thought about this. She said she did not know any Cecils. Nor did Angela, when she asked her. "Reactions to names are personal – and contingent, surely, on your background. Do you really think that everybody thinks the same about a Cecil, or a Cyril, I suppose?"

"Or Jules," Angela offered, ignoring the question. "Famous sportsmen called Jules? I don't think so. Jules is an interior decorator or, at a push, a chef."

"So, Georgia is . . ."

Angela smiled. "We'll find out. But I imagine she's self-confident. She's had things her way. She's assured." She looked at Julie, searching for confirmation. "You spoke to her – you must have formed an opinion."

"She seemed nice enough." It was all that Julie could find to say.

"I'm sure she is. Georgias usually are."

Julie was not sure whether Angela was entirely serious. She turned away from the window. The young woman they had been watching had crossed the street. "I'm going to let her in."

"Do you want me to see her too?" asked Angela.

Julie replied that of course she did. "You live here too."

"But it's your flat."

Julie was firm. "We're sharing. We live together – remember?"

Angela shrugged. "All right. We'll see. I'm sure she'll do. She could even be very nice. Who knows?"

It was Georgia's father who had first suggested that she should go to university in Edinburgh. He was a London orthopaedic surgeon with a lucrative practice, working in a private clinic favoured by wealthy foreigners. His nurse and his receptionists could speak four languages between them – they were his interpreters. He started in a very different sort of medicine, though, having trained in Edinburgh among colleagues who were disapproving of private medicine. Chance had taken him to London, when he undertook a locum appointment that unexpectedly became permanent. He had settled in a commuting town in Sussex after he married. His wife was an interior decorator and ran a business in the town's high street. They had two children, a boy and a girl. Georgia was born first, then there was Harry, who was asthmatic and struggled when the pollen count was high. There was asthma in the family, but Georgia had escaped it. She was good at sports, and distinguished herself in the expensive school to which they sent her. This was a girls' school, known for its high academic standards. She had done well, and had examination results that would have guaranteed her a place at most universities. She looked at Durham, which she liked for its atmosphere, but eventually chose Edinburgh, largely as a result of her father's persuasion.

The subject she chose to study was political theory. Edinburgh offered several courses that would have suited her, but she opted eventually for a course that concentrated on European political movements from the French Revolution onwards. There was a lot about the nineteenth century, and the processes of the Reform Movement. She also signed up for a course in Australian politics, offered by a colourful professor from Brisbane, who had a large personal following. She was now in the penultimate year of her four-year degree course, as were Julie and Angela. She had given no thought as to what she would do when she graduated. That had seemed a prospect so far off in the distance, but it was now beginning to seem a little closer. She would find something. She rather liked the idea of advertising. Her parents had a copy-writer friend who had once spoken to her about advertising as a career. This friend was proud of having come up with the slogan *Butter's best* for a major dairy firm. "It took three months," he'd said. "But it was worth the effort." Georgia had thought he was joking, but he had been quite serious. He, she knew, had a degree in philosophy from Cambridge. Perhaps that was where philosophy led. To the writing of copy. You did not have to have read the *Nicomachean Ethics* to say that butter was best, but perhaps you could then say it with some authority.

Although she had opted to study political theory, Georgia would not have described herself as being politically engaged. She had neither joined a political party nor voted in any election, even a local one, and was reluctant to slot herself into any obvious niche on the political spectrum. If pressed to state what she believed in, she would, reluctantly, say that she valued order. Anarchy, she said, was the real enemy – and it seemed to her that it was always there, lurking just out of sight, but ready to rear its unruly head and bring with it chaos and all sorts of suffering. Her parents were conservative in their instincts, and in their reading and voting habits too, and she had grown up without challenging their view of the world. And yet she did not want to be out of step with her contemporaries. Those, for the most part, were hostile to conservatism in any form, applying to themselves and those like them the description *progressive*. The causes they espoused were ones with which Georgia felt too embarrassed to identify herself publicly. She could see the arguments that lay behind them, but it was not her *style*, she felt, to take her place at their particular barricades. She was far too ready, a friend observed of her, to see both sides of an argument. That was not the way the world was, the friend said. We have oppressors and the oppressed; we have people who are sensitive to the feelings and needs of others, and then we have those who have no such sensitivity. You could not occupy a middle ground, this friend said – because there was no middle ground to occupy. It was too late for attempts to find compromise.

Because she was loathe to commit to a rigid interpretation of any issue or conflict, and because she believed that a sensible compromise could always be found to any problem, Georgia found herself agreeing with conservative positions on many issues. That was not out of any hard-heartedness or any failure of moral imagination on her part – it was more a result of her abhorrence for violence. She had read Burke on the French Revolution, and she felt it was inevitable that conflict would ensue if people took an extreme view of the issues that had been at play in that situation. Extremism meant that people got their heads chopped off, Georgia decided: tradition and caution were much safer, and less dangerous to good order. She was sure enough of that, but she was sensitive to the fact that it meant she was indeed out of step with so many of her contemporaries. They had posters of Che Guevara on their walls – that familiar bereted and bearded image that was pinned to countless student bedrooms. Nobody had Edmund Burke on their walls. That, she felt, was unfair: Burke had a strong distaste for injustice and for the suffering that was the lot of those at the bottom of the heap – his remedy, though, was not violence, but improvement at the instance of those in a position to do something about such failings. She had pointed this out in a university tutorial, but had been greeted with smiles from her fellow students. "But he's a conservative through and through," one of them said. "Everyone knows that." Another had looked at her with frank antipathy, saying, "I don't know how you can possibly believe that. Burke believed in the rights of those who exercised power at the time. It was that simple. That's conservatism, Georgia. Surely you can see that?"

Julie opened the door.

"I'm Georgia," Georgia said. "We spoke on the phone."

"Of course, we did."

She ushered her into the entrance hall, where Angela was waiting. Introductions were made. Julie noticed Angela's look of appraisal, as did Georgia, who glanced at Angela briefly before turning away.

"This is fabulous," said Georgia. "Light. Lots of room. And—"

"And the view?"

"Yes. The view," said Georgia. "Where I am at the moment," she went on, "I have a view of a tenement wall. And I see the windows at night. People in Tarvit Street tend not to use curtains. We see their dramas – live."

"There was a film like that," said Angela. "*Rear Window*. It was Hitchcock."

"I've seen it," said Georgia.

"What are you doing at uni?" asked Julie.

Georgia told them. She asked them about their courses, and they told her.

Then Julie asked her if she would like to see the room.

"You have a choice of three," she said.

"I'll take anything," said Georgia.

Angela laughed. "Are you desperate?"

Georgia nodded. "I'll die if you don't let me have the room. Seriously."

"Don't do that," said Julie. "It'll be fine by us. You can have the room. I'll tell you about the rent, though. If you're happy with that, then that's it."

"I'm not worried about the rent."

Angela thought: *her dad pays.* What must it be like to have that sort of support? *Yet, mine's paying too.* She was not sure how she felt about that. She had accepted parental help, yet she still felt slightly guilty about it.

They showed Georgia the rooms, and she chose one that was smaller than the other two, but which looked out over the Meadows. She stood at the window and gazed out over the trees. "I have a feeling that my life is about to start," she said. "All over again, that is."

Julie smiled. "Maybe it is," she said.

They made arrangements. Then, after Georgia left, Julie looked at Angela and said, "So?"

Angela shrugged. "She'll be all right."

"Just 'all right'?" asked Julie. "You don't sound very enthusiastic."

"It's not an audition," Angela responded. "You said you wanted to choose at random. So, she was first, and she got the room."

"But I hoped you'd at least *like* her."

"I didn't say I didn't," said Angela, a note of annoyance in her voice. "She's a type, isn't she? There are plenty of them. She's one. Privileged background. Everything on a plate. That's all. I just wondered whether people like that would fit in."

Julie looked thoughtful. "You don't think that *you* might be the one who's going to have trouble fitting in." She paused. "Do you disapprove of anybody who isn't like you? Just asking."

Angela swallowed. She turned from Julie's gaze. "I said that she was fine, and I mean it. I don't want to be awkward. I'll keep my views to myself, if you like."

Julie was conciliatory. "I'm sorry," she said. "I don't mean to criticise your views. I just want this to work. I want us to get along."

"We will," said Angela, and then she added, "Why shouldn't we?"

Five

My dearest friend

FIRST THERE WAS IAN, and then there was Neil. Ian
arrived on the day before Neil, and he chose the room next
to the room into which Georgia had just moved. There were
two rooms left unfilled – one being earmarked for Neil, and
the other for somebody yet to be chosen. According to Julie's
plan, that would be a man, as it remained her intention to have
an equal balance of the sexes. Angela had been less concerned
about that. "There'll be a couple of boys," she said. "Won't that
be enough?" It occurred to Julie that Angela was indifferent
to men. There was no evident sign of distaste, but she did
not seem enthusiastic. It was difficult: you could not ask the
obvious question directly, but it was there in the background,
all the more insistent for being unposed. She thought that
was where it should remain: people's preferences were their
own concern, and could remain private unless they chose to
declare them. That was common courtesy.

Ian had celebrated his twentieth birthday the day before he
moved in. He came from Perthshire, from a large farm twenty
miles from Dunkeld, a town in the hills to the north of Perth.
They lived on what was called a farm, although it could equally
well have been described as an estate. The description was an
act of self-definition, in a way: an estate had a social cachet
that a farm lacked. An estate proclaimed that its main purpose

was not the pedestrian raising of livestock or cultivating of crops – estates existed for the benefit of those who wanted to live a country existence. On estates, the practical work of agriculture was delegated rather than performed by the owner. Estates were also, in general, much larger than farms. In the Highlands of Scotland, estates were redolent of a past of dispossession, and of indifference to the claims of others. People used to live on those sprawling acreages, but had been put off the land to make way for the sporting moors, the scenic emptiness. A wound had been inflicted on a culture that had never recovered, and probably never would. Farms carried none of that harmful historical baggage.

Ian's father, Laurence, came from a Glasgow family of shipping brokers that had enjoyed modest prosperity in the period immediately before the Second World War. Their freight business had been taken over by a larger shipping concern, and Laurence had invested his share of the proceeds in a property that having once been called Glendonan Estate was now known as Glendonan Farm. The land had not been well-managed by its previous owner, and Laurence had to spend what spare funds he had on repairing buildings, sheds and byres that had fallen into disrepair. Fences, too, had been allowed to deteriorate, in many cases beyond the point of rescue. Some of the barbed wire used for fencing, it was rumoured, had been brought home from the trenches of the Somme and Ypres, and put to more pacific use on farms. Ian had been told that by his father, and had looked at the rolls of wire stacked in a shed after new fencing had been put in. Nobody knew what to do with it. A scrap metal merchant had considered it and decided it was not worth his trouble. "It should be treated as a war grave," he remarked. "Men died on that wire, you know."

Ian was eight when they moved from Glasgow to Glendonan. They had occupied a large Victorian house in Glasgow's West End prior to the move, and they had not been short of space. But now, in these hills, there was a spaciousness and freedom that he had never had before. There were two lochs, one of some size, the other more modest, but still large enough to have a boat moored off its banks and to support a population of brown trout. There were burns that ran off the hillside and, in one of these, a waterfall, a line of white that tumbled boyishly into a rock pool at its base. In the summer you could swim in this pool, even under the waterfall, which you would feel pounding on your head when the burn was in spate. There were deer that watched you, cautiously, nervously, before scattering off to higher ground. You could feel their eyes upon you, said Laurence. Their gaze was unflinching, even as their delicate forms seemed primed to dart off at the slightest sound or movement.

Ian was an only child. His mother, Natalie, had an ectopic pregnancy a couple of years after his birth, and had almost died. There had been further complications, and the prospect of her having another child had receded and then disappeared. She had been accepting of this, grateful to have survived the ectopic. She was an artist, and had set up a studio in one of the farm's outbuildings. It was a stark white room, with large skylights to catch the clear northern light that artists so appreciate. She painted the flora of the land about her: bog myrtle, wild orchids, the purple flowers of heather. There was a gallery in Edinburgh that showed her paintings and, with only the occasional exception, managed to sell them to specialist collectors. "There is nothing challenging about my art," she said. "I paint what I see. That's all. I don't try to improve on nature. Simple representation."

As a boy, Ian helped his father with the work of the farm. There was a farm manager and a tractor-man, and a general hand affectionately called the *orra man*, who took on tasks that nobody else wanted to do or could do. The orra man was taciturn, and often only smiled enigmatically in response to any remark addressed to him. "Aye, we'll see about that," was his usual answer to anything that required speech.

The nearest school was forty minutes away by road. They enrolled Ian there, and Natalie ferried him backwards and forwards each day. The road was narrow, and during the first winter they were there it was impassable on a number of occasions. At other times, there were patches prone to ice and it had to be negotiated painfully slowly. In the winter, too, their latitude dictated that the journey both ways was made in semi-darkness, as the sun rose after nine in the morning and set behind the hills to the west well before four each afternoon.

From her early twenties, Natalie had been prone to debilitating and recalcitrant depression. As the years passed, her bouts of illness became more frequent, each seeming to take a greater toll. She would sit in her studio, sometimes for hours, unable to begin a painting or take it beyond a few preliminary pencil strokes or daubs of paint. She sought treatment in Perth and in Edinburgh, and although anti-depressants brought some relief, and she was able to lead a normal life – and paint – for a period, the condition was always there in the background. "The black dog still hangs around," she said. "He never entirely goes away."

The strain of driving Ian to school every day made her increasingly anxious. Laurence offered to take over, but that did not allay her anxieties. She began to worry about what might happen to him on the roads, and no amount of reassurance could convince her that the chances of his being involved in an accident were remote. "You can't say that," she'd say. "Accidents happen all the time on those corners. You can't see what's coming."

After a year, the decision was taken that Ian should go off to a small prep school just outside Edinburgh. Boarding was put to him as an adventure, and he went along with the idea, although he was puzzled that his mother should not have objected. He could imagine that his father might have reasons to dispatch him to boarding school – he himself had been sent off at the age of ten and had boarded until he left school at eighteen. He said that he had enjoyed the experience, and had stayed in touch with his friends from those days. His mother had nothing like that in her background, and yet she raised no objection.

Laurence said, "You have to understand that your mother finds life very hard. It's not her fault, you know. It might be easier for her if she knows you are safe and sound at school. That might help her to feel a bit better, you see."

Ian said that he understood, although he had only the vaguest notion of what made life so difficult for his mother. Surely, she had everything she needed. She could do what she wanted to do, which was to paint; nobody was short of money, even if they had less than some people; everybody was nice to her and people gladly bought her artwork, too. Why should she worry about things that were never going to happen?

* * *

He spent two years at that small school. On the whole he was happy enough, although it was always a wrench leaving the farm at the end of the holidays. Shortly before he turned thirteen, he was sent to a larger boarding school, slightly closer to home, in a Perthshire glen. This involved a more difficult adjustment, as he was now one of six hundred rather than one of one hundred and fifty. And everybody, now, apart from those in his year, was older than he was, and more worldly-wise. There was bullying, mostly discreet and deniable by its perpetrators, but painful enough to its victims. There was homesickness, too, and an emphasis on sports that privileged those who were athletic. There were rules that seemed to him to make no sense at all, but the infringement of which led to arbitrary punishment.

He was singled out by an English teacher, a Walter Scott enthusiast, and by the age of sixteen he had made his way through all of the Waverley novels. He was encouraged to move on to Stevenson and then to the twentieth century. The English teacher gave him a copy of Robert Graves' *Goodbye to All That* and went on to encourage him to read Owen and Sassoon. "Why did they fight?" Ian asked. "Why didn't they refuse?" The teacher explained that prison was the alternative to conscription. He mentioned Douglas Young, the Scottish nationalist and classicist, who refused conscription by what he saw as an English parliament, and had been taken off to Saughton Prison, where he was serenaded from outside the prison walls by his nationalist friends playing the bagpipes. That was an exception; most people went without demur. "People thought they were doing the right thing," the teacher added. "Patriotism, you see. It distorts judgement. Not always, of course, but sometimes – if it's the wrong sort of patriotism."

The teacher had known Hugh MacDiarmid and had met Louis MacNeice. He spoke of the advantage of being able to say things in Scots. "A mundane thought sounds so much better in Scots," he said, half-seriously. He would have liked to be a poet, but had ended up teaching these middle-class Scottish boys who were, for the most part, indifferent to poetry. His life, it seemed, was a compromise between having to earn a living and hoping that one might be able to make a difference to some young life. He might strike a spark of something in the occasional imaginative pupil, but for the most part he felt he had no impact on their lives. They would go away in due course and forget about him and everything he had tried to instil in their minds. One or two of them might remember some scraps here and there. He had encountered one of his graduates years after he had left school, who had greeted him with *April is the cruellest month*. He had said that he'd never forgotten that line.

He knew that the boys had a nickname for him – they called him The Buffalo, for reasons he had been unable to fathom fully, but that might have had something to do with his moustache. He lived with his wife and young daughter in one of the staff houses. The boys called it The Buffalo Pen.

For Ian, there were friendships, too. A boy in his year invited him to his father's house on Skye, and the parents of another friend included him on their family holiday in a rented villa on Corfu. They knew about his mother's depression, and were sympathetic. "Be kind to Ian," his friend's mother told her son. "When people struggle with that condition over time, it can end badly. In extreme cases, that is, but I gather that Ian's mother is quite seriously affected."

That was true, and the depressive episodes became deeper and more prolonged. Shortly after his sixteenth birthday, his housemaster called him in one afternoon from a game of football and broke the news that his mother had been admitted to hospital in Perth. His father had telephoned to say that he was coming to see him and was expected to arrive within the hour. The housemaster was able to tell him no more than that, but Ian was sure that his father would be coming to give him bad news. Why else would he come in person, rather than use the telephone? The end of a world is best announced face-to-face, of course – that must be the reason.

The housemaster tried to be positive. "They can do so much these days to help people in your mother's position," he said. "I'm sure she'll be all right."

He knew, though, from his father's expression when he arrived that the news was as he had feared it would be. His father embraced him, wordlessly at first. Ian wanted to ask what had happened, but before he could say anything his father said, "It all became too painful for her. She couldn't help herself."

He did not ask for any details, but reflected, in silence, on the last time he had seen her, which was just before his father drove him back to school. He had gone into the studio and seen her sitting before a half-finished watercolour of a lichen-covered rock. She had said, "People ignore lichen, you know. They walk past it without thinking of the miracle."

He had said, "I really like it. You make it look so lovely."

"But that's what it is – it's lovely. Like just about everything in this country."

His father had called to him to hurry up. They should not be late.

He had kissed his mother. She touched him gently on the shoulder in a gesture, he thought, of sympathy, as if to say that she knew what it was like to leave home and face the rigours of boarding school. She did not know that, he told himself. His father knew all about it, but her experience had been different. And then they were driving along the bumpy farm road, down towards the junction with the public road. He thought he saw her standing at the studio window, but it might have been a trick of the light. What he thought was his last glimpse of her, then, might have been no more than an illusion. Sometimes we have only shadows to remember.

When he returned to the school ten days later, there was a note on the desk in the study he shared with four others. It was in an envelope on which his name was written. He recognised the writing as that of his friend Stewart, with whose family he had gone to Greece the previous year.

He put the envelope in a pocket, to open it later that day, after the evening homework period. He did so outside, and read it while standing with his back to the hills overlooking the school, its guardians. The evening sky was still light and somewhere, in the distance, the school's pipers could be heard practising. The sound of the pipes carried so far in that pure, sharp air, up to the sky, the notes reverberating against the walls of the quad before they died away at the end of the measure. They played *Highland Cathedral* again and again; they never tired of it. There was a rugby match the following day, and they would play it before kick-off.

My dearest friend, he read. *I am so sorry about what happened. Your heart must be broken. I am thinking of you. As always, Stewart.*

He read it again. *My dearest friend . . .* The words were powerful in their comfort. *My dearest friend . . .* He had not thought that he was a dearest friend to anybody, but now he was. Here it was, expressed in those three words. He took the letter out and read it again, lingering on the opening. Three words could change everything. He looked up at the sky, at that moment an entirely complicit witness to what he felt.

Six

Flatmates and lovers

NEIL ARRIVED WITH ALL his possessions packed into two suitcases, one of which was bursting at the seams.

"These are all my worldly goods," he said. "I'm not exaggerating – this is the lot. This is everything I own."

Julie said, "What do they say about travelling light through life?"

Neil shrugged. "That you should do it?"

"Yes."

He looked at his suitcases. He noticed that Angela's eyes were on him. The suitcases were not very impressive, but then, how much *stuff* did one need? As a boy, he had seen a photograph of Mahatma Gandhi's possessions when he died: a pair of wire-rimmed glasses, sandals, a dhoti and a pocket watch. That was about it. And yet he was carried off to his funeral pyre on the shoulders of thousands. That was what counted.

Not that he aspired to Eastern asceticism. He would like to go to India one day, and would do so, he hoped. He would make a pilgrimage to one of those holy rivers and be washed clean of all his sins, not that he had had the opportunity to commit many so far. There was always time, though. Of course, you had to be careful about those rivers. Don't swallow any of the water, because if you did you would be seriously ill.

Julie eyed the suitcases. "There's a massive cupboard in your room," she said. "There's plenty of space."

He had phoned the previous day, having seen the notice in the Student Union. He had said he would take the room sight unseen, so keen was he to find somewhere. "I have a room in a house in Leith," he said. "It's tiny. A cupboard, really. My landlady fusses a lot. She goes on about how I use all the hot water – which I don't, by the way."

Julie laughed. "I'm not a landlady. I'm a flatmate."

"Of course."

"So, can I reserve it?"

She said that he could, and the deal was done.

The suitcases were put into the room that would be Neil's, and they went into the kitchen, where Julie offered to make him coffee.

"I don't really know anything about you," she said. "Perhaps you could tell me."

"And I don't know anything about you," said Neil. "Or . . ." He nodded towards the door through which Angela had returned to her room.

"Angela. Okay. You tell me first."

Neil sat down at the kitchen table. "I'm doing architecture. Third year."

"Architecture goes on for ever, doesn't it?"

"We go off to work in a firm for a year – and then we come back. You eventually get registration, but it takes a long time."

"You don't want buildings to fall down, do you?"

"True. A lot of it is mundane, you know. Strength of materials and so on. Positioning doors. Stuff like that isn't exactly—"

"Glamorous?"

"Yes. People like Basil Spence or le Corbusier don't have to worry about where the doors will go. That's the sort of architect I'd like to be, but it won't happen."

She looked at him. You could not really take people in properly when you met them first; you had to wait for an opportunity to observe them. You may notice prominent cheekbones at first glance, or an unusual eye colour; you may get an impression of regularity of features; but real assessments come later, when you notice things you might have missed. As they sat in the kitchen, Julie found it difficult not to stare at Neil. At first, he seemed unaware of her gaze, but then, in the middle of saying something, he paused, as if he was puzzled by her interest.

She was flustered. "You said you come from Orkney?"

He nodded. "Yes. Have you ever been there?"

She said that she had visited the islands with a friend a few years ago. "My friend had an aunt up there. We stayed with her and went to the music festival in Kirkwall."

"The St Magnus Festival?"

"Yes. And afterwards, we spent a few days on the main island. We went to Stromness – and some of those prehistoric sites, the brochs."

"And the chapel built by the Italian prisoners-of-war?"

She had seen that. "I found it rather moving. Those men were all that way from home and they made a chapel out of bits and pieces. An Italian chapel so far from Italy."

He smiled. "They got on so well with everybody. The prisoners weren't really locked up. They helped the locals and the locals helped them."

"I'm not sure the Italians were all that enthusiastic about the Second World War."

Neil agreed. "They had far better things to do than fight. Mussolini was an aberration. He had the national love of smart uniforms and bravado. But they didn't really have the heart for it. Italians find it relatively difficult to be nasty."

"But they were – to an extent."

"Yes, to an extent. Every country has its bullies, and there were enough of them to come out of the woodwork."

She asked him where he would do his year out – the year he had to spend working in an architect's office. That was simple, he said: his father had an architectural practice on the island, in Kirkwall. It had always been assumed that he would do the year in the family firm.

"And go back and work there?" she asked. "After you graduate?"

Neil hesitated. "It doesn't sound very adventurous, does it?" he said. "But yes. Part of me says go off and work in London or Berlin, or somewhere like that, but then another part tells me I'll always be happier in Orkney. That's where I'm from. It's the place I love, I suppose." He looked at her enquiringly. "Is there anywhere that you really love? Not just like – but actually love?"

She thought for a moment. "We've lived where we've lived – my family, that is – for four generations. We still live there. It's in East Lothian – about fifteen miles away. It's home, and yes, I love it." She paused. "But I love Scotland too."

Neil nodded. "So do I. But I wonder whether we're being a bit – how should I put it? – a bit stick-in-the-mud? Aren't people meant to want to go out into the world? Aren't we meant to enjoy discovering new places, new sights, and so on?"

She shrugged. "Did you read Hugh MacDiarmid at school up in Orkney?"

Neil frowned. "A bit. For my Highers. We read *Island Funeral*."

"Do you remember what he wrote about the rose of all the world? Remember: he didn't want the rose of all the world, he just wanted the little white rose of Scotland that smelled sharp and sweet and—"

"Can break the heart? Something like that?"

"Exactly."

She looked at him. She had not imagined that so shortly after meeting they would be having a conversation like this about things that mattered. So many conversations in the early stages of an acquaintanceship remained at a superficial level. They had been talking about love of place, of country – serious, important subjects that she had always enjoyed discussing. The problem was, though, that people were often unwilling to talk about them, preferring the usual small talk. She looked away, concerned that he might see in her expression the feeling that had rather suddenly come upon her. *Don't*, she said to herself. *Don't allow yourself. He's your new flatmate. Don't.*

They had been sitting in the kitchen, talking over the coffee that she had made. Now she stood up. "You'll want to unpack."

He stood up too. Then he said, "Is that everybody then – the people you told me about? Angela, Georgia, and—"

"Ian. No. This flat is vast. There are six bedrooms. There's one still to be filled."

He asked her who it would be.

"I'm not sure," she said. "I'll know tomorrow."

"Are there any special rules?" he asked. "You know how some flats have special rules. No music after eleven – that sort of thing."

She shook her head. "There's nothing."

"And people to stay?" he asked. "I don't mean long-term . . ."

Her discomfort showed. "You mean staying overnight?"

He shifted on his feet. "Just asking."

The tension that had arisen with his question dissipated quickly. "Personal lives are private," she said. "What I don't think we should have is people moving boyfriends or girlfriends into the flat. This is a flat for six, not for twelve."

He laughed. "Of course."

She turned away. She had felt a sudden stab of jealousy. It was unexpected, but it was real enough – and painful. She did not like the thought that he would find a girlfriend. It was as simple – and as possessive – a feeling as that.

The following day, Julie left the flat early, before any of the others, except for Neil, who had told them that he regularly started the day with a visit to the gym. Halfway through the morning, in the library coffee bar, she saw Angela, sitting reading by herself.

"If that's important," Julie said, "I'll go away."

Angela closed the book with a sigh. "My nineteenth-century novel course. This book isn't going to end well."

"They loved their tragedy, the Victorians. They were very—"

"Melodramatic?"

"Yes." Julie paused. "Unlike us. We're realists. We don't really go in for the grand gesture. Or romance, for that matter."

Angela frowned. "Romance is alive and well. I went into our local library a few weeks ago. They have a shelf for recently returned books. What's on it, do you think?"

Julie knew the answer. "Those bodice-rippers? Doctor and nurse romances?"

"Right on both counts," said Angela. "There were tons of them. But there were other books too. *A History of Greece*, for example."

Julie nodded.

"You're surprised?" asked Angela. Her tone was slightly defensive, and Julie was glad she had not said anything.

"No. Libraries have to cater to all tastes."

Angela agreed. But the defensiveness came out once more. "There's a strong tradition of self-education in mining communities, you know."

Julie tilted her head in agreement. There was a Scottish tradition of education. That was still there.

"There are people who never had the chances we have," Angela went on. "But they educate themselves if they can. Some of my own family have done that."

Julie said she knew about that. "I admire that," she said. Then, after a pause, she said, "I hope you don't think that I'm not aware of the struggle that many people have. I am, you know."

Angela looked embarrassed. "I'm sorry," she said. "I wasn't accusing you of anything. I know that you're not like some of these people." She cast a quick glance around the crowd of students in the coffee room. It was possibly a bit harsh, Julie thought, but it was true that there would have been many in the room who had enjoyed real advantage.

But then Angela appeared to have second thoughts. "I'm not writing them off," she muttered, seeming tense. "Maybe I shouldn't be so quick to judge others."

Julie laughed. "Don't worry. I didn't think you were."

Angela relaxed a little again. "Those romantic novels," she said. "The ones you see in supermarkets. Have you ever read one?"

Julie admitted that she had. "I read two a few years back. They were on the shelves of the place we were staying in."

"The covers say everything there is to be said," Angela continued. "The hero always looks the same. Drop-dead gorgeous."

"Like Neil," said Julie.

It slipped out. She had not intended to say it, but she had. And now Angela looked up sharply. A grin broke across her face. "I wasn't going to say anything." Her grin widened. "But since you bring the subject up – yes, he's very nice-looking. You didn't choose him because of that, did you?"

Julie reminded her that there had been no choosing at all. "I told you – no selection."

"Yes, I remember!" Angela laughed. "Well, it worked rather well in this case. He's sweet."

"Good." She thought that sweet was not a word that Angela would have used. Was it condescending? What were the implications of *sweet*?

Julie waited. When it seemed that Angela had nothing to add, she said, "You'd think that somebody like him would be snapped up."

Angela pursed her lips. "He might not be interested."

Julie thought about this. Then she said, "I don't think it's that. I think if anything, he's a bit reserved."

"You mean, shy?"

She did not think that shy was quite the right word. She had meant what she said: Neil was reserved. It was different.

For a few moments there was a pause in the conversation. At the table next to theirs, three students, a young man and two young women, were engaged in a discussion that was becoming increasingly heated. "We shouldn't accept what they're trying to do," said the young man. "They're trying to dismantle the state."

"I don't think so," said one of the young women, glancing in embarrassment at the neighbouring tables. "There are two sides to it."

The argument went back and forth. Angela caught Julie's eye, and made a face. Julie looked at her watch. She had a lecture to get to, and after that she was going to return to the flat.

She said to Angela, "Our next flatmate is coming to see me at five this evening. He's called James. Will you be around?"

Angela took a final sip of her coffee. "I could be."

"Neil will be in," he said. "Georgia, too. We can have a whole committee."

"Who is he anyway?"

"He sounded American on the phone. Or Canadian."

"Interesting."

As they got up from the table, somebody waved to Angela from the other side of the room. Angela acknowledged the wave, but not, thought Julie, with much warmth. She saw that Julie had noticed, and she muttered under her breath. "Can't stand her."

Julie glanced across the room. A rather plain young woman in dungarees sat at a table by herself. Her face was slightly freckled. She had an eager, open expression.

"Who is she?" she asked.

"Nobody," replied Angela. She looked away.

This response made Julie feel uncomfortable. Nobody, in her view, deserved to be called nobody.

Seven

Do you make mayonnaise?

A T THREE O'CLOCK THAT afternoon, the flat's buzzer sounded. This was operated from the doorway to the common stair, down on the ground floor. That front door could be opened by the pressing of a button in each of the flats, an intercom system allowing householders to speak to callers before admitting them.

It was not James, who was not due until five, but a young woman who introduced herself simply as Lizzie.

"You don't know me," she said through the intercom. "But I know Mrs Donald."

It took Julie a moment or two to remember who Mrs Donald was. Then it came back to her.

"She said I should have a word with you. Do you mind?"

Julie pressed the button to open the stair door and went out to the landing to await her visitor. Down below she heard the creak of the front door on its hinges, followed by the sound of footsteps on the stone stairway. She stood back: it would be disconcerting for a visitor to look up and see herself being gazed down upon.

Lizzie appeared at the top of the stairs. She was, thought Julie, about her own age, on the thin side, with an attractive, rather waif-like face. Her clothes were unexceptional: a pair of blue jeans and a cheesecloth top: a version of the uniform of her age group.

"I'm Lizzie," she said, offering to shake hands with Julie. "And I know you weren't expecting me."

"That's all right," said Julie. "You said that Mrs Donald . . ."

She did not finish. "She spoke to me yesterday," Lizzie interjected. "She said that I should get in touch as soon as possible."

Julie led her into the sitting room. Angela was there, and had now been joined by Ian. They introduced themselves to Lizzie. Julie invited their visitor to sit down.

"I'm looking for a room in a flat," Lizzie said. "Mrs Donald said you had told her that you might have something here. She said you were looking for a few people."

She looked at Julie imploringly.

Julie said, "How do you know her?"

"I clean her flat for her," replied Lizzie. "I do two sessions for her each week. It's not my main job."

Ian had said nothing. Now he asked, "Are you a student?"

Lizzie blushed. "Me? No." She lowered her gaze. "I never went to college or anything like that. I'm doing an apprenticeship instead."

Ian looked interested. "What in?"

"Catering. I work in a hotel. You probably know it. The one at the end of Princes Street – above Waverley Station. I was at Gleneagles for a while – a year and a bit. Then I transferred."

They heard this in silence. Then Angela said, "And at the end of it? What will you be at the end? A chef?"

Lizzie nodded. "Yes. I'll have the basic qualification. They move us from department to department, you see. You spend months just making soup or whatever. You build up experience in as many different bits of the kitchen as possible."

Angela said, "Useful. You'll always get a job, I suppose."

Lizzie said she thought that was so. "It's hard work, though."

Julie cleared her throat. "I'm really sorry to disappoint you," she said. "But we're not looking for any flatmates."

Lizzie looked immediately crestfallen. "No room?"

"Not quite yet," said Angela.

But at the same time, Julie said, "Yes, we're full."

Lizzie looked from Angela to Julie, and then back again.

"I mean, we've got somebody lined up for the room," Julie said hurriedly.

Lizzie was silent. After a few moments, she stood up. "I'm too late, then?"

"I'm sorry," said Julie. "Will you tell Mrs Donald that we would have liked to help?"

Lizzie nodded, but did not say anything further, other than to announce that she had to get to the hotel for her evening shift.

Julie was looking at her; her expression was one of slight puzzlement. "Do you make mayonnaise?" she asked. "Is that the department you're in?"

Lizzie looked at her with astonishment. "Did I say anything about mayonnaise?"

"No," said Julie. "I just wondered." She did not say that she had detected the smell of mayonnaise on Lizzie's clothing. It was a strong smell, and strong smells could adhere to fabrics. Cigarette smoke was one example; mayonnaise, it seemed, was another.

"Because I'm the mayonnaise assistant at the North British Hotel right now. I do some sauces – I'm learning those too – but they put me on mayonnaise because I seem to be able to do that."

"Mayonnaise is tricky, isn't it?" said Ian. "It curdles, doesn't it?"

"Yes," said Lizzie.

Ian was surprised to hear that one person could be kept busy in a full-time job making mayonnaise.

"It's a big kitchen," said Lizzie. "And I do other things. But look, I'm sorry – I'm going to have to go."

James was slightly older than the others – he was a month short of his twenty-third birthday. He was also already a graduate, and was now enrolled on a one-year master's course in the university's department of philosophy. He had been born in Massachusetts, he said, but had lived in New York since he was fifteen.

He sat in the kitchen with Julie. Angela had gone out – she had a salsa class and had decided that it took priority. "I'll meet him when he moves in," she had said. "And we're not interviewing him, are we? So it makes no difference."

Julie looked at James over the top of her coffee cup. He met her gaze. "You probably want to know something about me," he said. "If I'm going to be living here—"

"I need to know that you can pay the rent," said Julie.

He laughed. "Sure. No problem. And my share of any other bills."

Julie said that they would share the electricity bill. Between six of them it should not be too much.

"And I'll pull my weight," said James. "Cleaning and so on."

"You're obviously house-trained," said Julie.

"I shared an apartment in my senior year," said James. He looked about him. "It was nothing like this. This is luxury." He paused. "I'll tell you about myself – if you're interested."

Julie assured him that she was. "There's not much to say about me," she said. "You've probably done much more than I have."

"We always think that other people are more interesting than we are," said James. "But often they aren't." He paused. "Okay, me. I told you that I came from Massachusetts. There's a town called Concord. That's where we lived.

"My dad was a high school principal. He did that for years, and then he had his great break. He had an uncle who had a speakers' bureau in New York. He had been in the music business – he booked singers and session players – and then he decided to start representing speakers. He had this guy called Larry Buckle – that wasn't a stage name – and he gave a talk, with slides – *How to Marry Money*. I'm not making this up. That was his line, and he was really popular. People flocked to his talk. They sat there and took notes. They seriously hoped to pick up tips on how to attract a wealthy partner.

"Apparently, Larry had come down in the world. He had once married money, but money had divorced him, and all he got from it was a condo in Boca Raton. That's down in Florida and it's a place full of people who have married money or even made some of it themselves, although that's a bit harder, of course.

"Larry Buckle, though, was only the beginning. He found a tennis star who had hit a losing streak and so wanted to get on the lecture circuit. Then he picked up a whole lot of authors who had written books on just about everything. He sent them off on the circuit – to give their talks at libraries and country clubs and conventions. And he did pretty well out of it. But he was getting on and Larry Buckle had persuaded him to buy a condo next door to his in Boca Raton, and so he retired and went down there. He passed the business on to my dad. That was ten years ago. Then he – my uncle, that is – died two years ago and my dad was left in full control of the business. He runs it now with my mom, who proved to be really good at it. I helped them a bit last summer, booking hotels for the speakers and so on.

"Uncle Ed had no kids. He had already handed on the speakers' bureau and that left the place in Boca Raton and the money in his savings account. He left the condo to Larry Buckle's sister, who was a professional bridge player. They had been having an on-off affair for years – I think they both felt sorry for one another – and he thought he had some responsibility for her. Her eyesight was beginning to go and she was playing the wrong cards. He left the money in the savings account to me. It wasn't a vast sum, but it will be enough to buy an apartment somewhere if I want, with a bit left over. I decided to use the bit left over to come over here and do a graduate degree. And that's what I'm doing. But I have to find somewhere to live. I'm staying in a bed-and-breakfast place at the moment, which I don't like. So here I am.

"Oh, I didn't tell you what I do. I did philosophy at Dartmouth College. There's a great philosophy programme there, and it was just right for me. I wanted to carry on because philosophy is the thing that interests me more than anything else. I know that in most cases it leads nowhere – you can teach it – if you're lucky enough to get a job – but apart from that, you have to earn your living some other way. That's okay with me. I could end up running the speakers' bureau, I suppose, or teaching high school or something, but the point is that I will have at least studied what I want to study – I will have had that chance."

He paused, at last, and looked enquiringly at Julie. "What do you do, by the way?"

"History of art."

He spread his hands. "There. Same thing. It's not far removed from philosophy. Aesthetic theory is philosophy, after all."

"I know. I love that stuff."

James grinned. "Perhaps we see the world in the same way."

"Perhaps."

He waited. Julie had made up her mind – or made it up more than it had been made before he arrived. She liked James. She'd enjoyed his story, its matter-of-fact details and sometimes odd family connections. There was a gentleness about him that appealed to her. Yet it was not weakness. Decency, perhaps? Sometimes it was difficult, she thought, to determine exactly why we liked some people and disliked others. Dislike was easier to rationalise, though, because it tended to be founded on observed characteristics: selfishness, pushiness, prudishness – there was a long list of things to dislike about people. Liking, though, was fuzzier, and more difficult to tie to a particular reason.

But she moved on to discuss the rent, which he said he found entirely reasonable. "I would have paid more," he said. "If you had asked, that is."

She showed him the room. He was the last to arrive, and so it was the least spacious. But he said he had been in New York apartments where the bedrooms were much smaller. "And this place has got light," he said. "Look out there. Look at that sky. That's north, isn't it?"

"Yes."

"Clear light, then. Northern light is what artists look for. And philosophers too, I believe."

She said that he could have as much Scottish light as he wished.

"It's the same light that made everything so clear for David Hume," said James, as he stood by the window. "Perhaps there really was something in the light that made Hume and his friends see things so clearly. After all, it was the Scottish Enlightenment . . ." He turned and smiled at her. "Sorry," he said. "A photon is just a photon. All photons are equal."

She said that she was not sure about photons. "One day we could talk about colours, though. I have views on colour. On blue, for instance. Blue is a very important colour in art history, you know. The pigment was expensive."

"Yes," said James. "One day we can talk about blue." He looked thoughtful. "There's a great book – a philosophical inquiry – on the subject. *On Being Blue*. Have you read it?"

She admitted that she had not. There was so much that she had not read that she had no idea where to start. It was easy to feel defeated when you thought of the things you did not know.

"It's by a guy called William Gass. He trained as a philosopher, you know. He actually studied under Wittgenstein when he was at Cornell." He gave her an enquiring look. You could not count on people knowing who Wittgenstein was, and he thought perhaps she might not.

But she nodded, and said, "Wittgenstein? Really?" She knew that Wittgenstein was a philosopher, but he could equally well have been a place in Central Europe, or even a beer from such a place.

He smiled, and then glanced at his watch. "Can we discuss

THE PRIVATE SIDE *of* FRIENDSHIP

blue some other time?" he said. He had to see somebody about
something and would she mind if he left in a few minutes?
There was something to be settled, though, before he left. "So
that's definite?" he said. "If you'll have me, that is."

"Of course we will."

He could tell that she meant it, and he was pleased. It was
not always easy being in a foreign country; one could never
be sure that one was reading people correctly. There were
potential misunderstandings, and one never knew just when
they might occur.

They shook hands.

He said, "The handshake is universal, isn't it?"

She laughed. "I think so," she said. "Except if you're a Pacific
Islander. They rub noses, I believe."

"Oh," he said. "That's a nice way of doing things too."

She saw him to the door. She had been pleased by the
encounter. She had been prepared to come up with some
pretext for not offering him the room had her reaction to him
been a negative one, but she had felt no reservations at all.
James was easy, comfortable company. His manner could be
described as agreeable – a word that summed up the quality
of being in agreement. Agreeable people were easy to get
on with because they looked for harmony in their dealings
with others. Agreeable people were not disputatious – they
wanted comity above all else. It would be a pleasure having
James about the flat, with all his agreeableness. James would
be *comforting*.

Before he left, Julie said, "There was something you said."

They were at the front door of the flat. The atmosphere in
the stairwell was cooler than the air in the flat. She felt it
touch her face. Somewhere downstairs, probably in the flat

immediately below theirs, somebody was cooking curry. The smell, drifting up the stair, was quite strong, and she felt she should apologise to James. "We don't usually get cooking smells from neighbours," she said.

He frowned, and she realised that he had not noticed the smell.

"I pick that sort of thing up," she said. "I have a good sense of smell. It can be a bit of a disadvantage sometimes."

"I can imagine."

"One thing I wanted to ask you," she said. "When you were talking about the business back home – the speakers' bureau."

"Yes?"

"You talked about that man called Larry Buckle."

"Yes. Larry."

She asked him whether he had ever met him. "He sounds so . . . well, so awful. Going round talking about how to marry money . . . It just sounds so . . . so tacky."

James laughed. "But it was. Tacky's not strong enough. It was . . . more than tacky. And did I meet him? Yes – often. Usually with my uncle."

"What was he like? I mean, to look at?"

James thought for a few moments. "Imagine a dance instructor from an old black and white movie. A natty dresser. Centre parting." He raised an eyebrow. "Can you see him?"

She grinned. "Yes."

"That was Larry Buckle."

"Thank you."

He turned to leave. She closed the door and went back into the flat. As she did so, she thought, *I've made this happen. I've got this group of people together.* She did not think in self-congratulatory terms – it was easy enough to fill the rooms of a flat in a university city. What struck her was the fact that she had brought a series of parallel lives to a confluence, and this could have a profound effect on some, or even all of them. Now that they were all under the same roof, nothing, for each of them, would ever be the same.

Julie stopped. An unexpected thought came to her. She might become involved with one of these young men. She wanted to. Everybody else, it seemed to her, was experienced, and she was not. She was not going to allow herself to become what a previous generation would have called an old maid. One of these days, she said to herself, I am going to have to take that particular step.

She felt embarrassed at her own thoughts – at what amounted to a private concupiscence. It was ridiculous to be so calculating. Love was not a matter of taking a decision. Love involved being overcome by feeling; you *fell* in love – an expression which described the involuntary nature of the experience. Love was insidious, the realisation that one was in love usually coming as a surprise. Even if it had happened to you before, you might still be unprepared.

Eight

April 1984

Can we talk about this in my room?

A FEW WEEKS LATER, Georgia and Julie found themselves the only people in the flat one evening. Angela had a part-time job in a bar that involved her being out for two evenings each week – and this was one of them. James had gone down to London for two days to meet a friend from the States who was passing through on his way to Prague, and Ian and Neil had gone to a folk evening in one of the pubs on the South Side. A band from Orkney was performing that night, and Neil had been sent a couple of tickets.

Georgia was late with an essay, as she often seemed to be. She had taken a break and was making herself a coffee in the kitchen when Julie came in. "Alternative voting systems in parliamentary democracies," she intoned. "Can you think of a sexier topic than that? A whole essay on single transferable vote systems and so on. And I *sound* so dull. On the one hand, there is this, and on the other—"

"Perhaps being even-handed is always going to be dull," said Julie. "I don't like to quote Yeats too often . . ."

"Hah! So modest."

"But sometimes, you have to. What did Yeats say? The

best lack all conviction and the worst are full of passionate intensity. Something like that."

Georgia agreed. "It's hard to be passionate about voting systems, but some people are, I suppose. Not me, though." She paused. "Art history's different. People get very worked up over paintings, don't they?"

"Oh, sure. They feel very moved. They cry." She remembered the trip to the Uffizi – the one where her father had been so ill with food-poisoning. She had seen a woman weeping in front of *The Birth of Venus*. Sobbing. And she had watched her, when others had turned away, as if unwilling to intrude on a private grief. It was so far removed from the dry discussions of the lecture room.

She continued, "And yet some art historians are so . . . *controlled*. Perhaps that's the word. Almost cold."

Georgia looked thoughtful. "Are you thinking of Anthony Blunt?"

Julie was unsure. "Blunt?"

"He was the Director of the Courtauld Institute. Surveyor of the Queen's Pictures. And—"

"Oh, the spy? He was the one who'd been a Soviet spy? The newspapers were full of it."

Georgia nodded. "That was him. He died last year. Last March."

"I think I saw an interview he gave," said Julie. "He was on television. He sat there hardly blinking an eyelid. He was very composed."

Georgia hesitated. There was something she was not sure she should tell Julie. But now she decided. "He was a cousin. A very distant one, but we were actually related. It was explained to me once what the connection was, but I've forgotten. It's remote, anyway."

Julie looked at her in astonishment. "You mean . . ."

"Yes, my mother called him Cousin Anthony. She saw quite a bit of him when she was younger – at family occasions, that sort of thing. He was a bit older than she is. Almost twenty years, in fact."

"And did you know him yourself? Did you see him?"

"Sometimes at weddings and funerals. He was a rather quiet man. He was soft spoken and very elegant. You felt that if you bumped into him, you'd shatter him. He was always very polite. He never needed to be reminded of my name. That surprised me, because, as I said, we were only very distantly related. Fourth cousins or something. He gave me a copy of a book he wrote on Poussin. I've got it at home."

Julie was impressed. She liked Poussin, and Anthony Blunt had been the authority on his work. Poussin was controlled, of course: he was, some felt, a rather cold observer. His paintings were very classical, very posed.

She gave Georgia a sideways look. "And the fact that he was a Russian spy? What did the family think of that?"

Georgia remembered the day her parents had learned that Cousin Anthony had been an agent of Moscow from the late thirties until after the War. Her father had reacted with cold anger. "He could have compromised D-Day," he said. "He passed on information to the Soviet intelligence services when everybody knew how leaky they were. He knew that the Nazis had penetrated them. He was a traitor pure and simple."

Her mother had been more sympathetic. "He acted out of conscience. He felt he had to tell the Russians what was being kept from them."

Her father was unimpressed. "Nonsense."

"Those men, the Cambridge Five, thought that the only people standing up to Fascism were the Russians."

This brought an even stronger reaction. "Who were, incidentally, in a pact with the Nazis – at least at the beginning."

"The left may have been naïve about the Soviet Union – and about Stalin – but they meant well. Remember it was the thirties. Hunger marches and so on. They thought they had no choice."

Her father had muttered about Blunt not having gone to live in Moscow – unlike Philby or Burgess. "Too effete," he said. "He would never have survived there. Moscow was no place for pansies."

"It wasn't that simple," said her mother. "And I'd prefer you not to use that horrid word, thank you. Anthony was . . . extremely artistic. That's not the same thing, you know."

Georgia had not been part of this conversation, but she had heard every word. She knew what her mother meant: her father did not understand men like Anthony Blunt. He thought that an interest in art was somehow fundamentally unmasculine, like being keen on ballet, he always said. She and her mother, she had decided, had a similar taste in men: they both liked men who were sensitive, perhaps a little feminine. And yet her mother had married her father, with his full-blown alpha-male personality. All surgeons were like that, she had heard. They're assertive, even to the point of being bullies in theatre. They were forceful and inclined to think they were right about everything.

There were some respects in which her parents' marriage puzzled her. Why had her mother married him if he was the opposite of what she admired? Because she was encouraged by ambitious parents, she thought. Her grandparents, in spite of one or two grand connections – Blunt was very well-placed – were not particularly well-off. A surgeon represented security. It never occurred to them to free themselves of that financial ambition, and neither did it occur to her mother.

Now, Julie said to Georgia, "I can't imagine what it's like – having a relative who was the subject of such attention – and dislike."

"I never disliked him," said Georgia.

"But you had no reason to," said Julie. "He had a brilliant public career, and he was family to you. That excuses just about everything – usually. Whereas there were others to whom he stood for the impunity that class gives you in this country. If you speak with the right accent and know the right people, you can always do what you like." She paused. "Blunt stood for that sort of privilege."

"They rounded on him."

Julie sighed. "Of course they did. What do you expect? There is nothing that this country likes better than a witch-hunt. It's in the nation's genes, I think. What has always been one of the most hackneyed images of English life? The hunt riding to hounds." She wrinkled her nose in disgust. "All those otherwise rational adults, dressed in scarlet, charging across the countryside after some wretched frightened creature – that they propose to kill by ripping him to shreds. There have always been people who love that sort of thing."

Georgia shared Julie's distaste. "I hate the idea of hunting – any hunting. I always have."

"I don't like it either," said Julie. "How can anyone take pleasure in the killing of another creature? At snuffing out a life – even a small life, like the life of a bird?" She paused. "The Italians shoot swallows, you know. They stand there, with their guns, and as the swallows fly overhead on their journey, they blast them out of the sky."

Georgia was still thinking about witch-hunts. Julie was right, she thought: campaigns of that sort were a popular pursuit. And the braying mob was nothing new: it was often how humanity bonded. The witch-hunter's job was to remind us that we were unsettled by dissent, by the existence of those who might be unlike us, or unlike what we took ourselves to be. The Spanish Inquisition. The Dreyfus affair in France. McCarthyism in America. There was example after example in which we searched for people to blame so that we could feel more assured, or stronger, or more righteous.

Julie looked at Georgia. "Would you have turned him in if you had found out? I mean, if you had discovered that this distant cousin of yours was a Soviet spy, and nobody knew – would you have gone to the authorities? Or would your loyalty to him have stood in the way?"

It was a question that Georgia had already asked herself – on more than one occasion after Anthony Blunt's exposure. She had little hesitation in answering it now. She would not have betrayed him. It was an old battle, she decided: business from a long time ago that had nothing to do with her and with her generation. And what was the point in punishing an elderly man, in shaming him for something that had happened forty or more years ago? Would it make any material difference to anybody?

She met Julie's stare. "I don't think so." She remembered what Cousin Anthony himself had said when he was interviewed by *The Times*. He had told them that he could never betray his friends – which meant that he would never have given up Burgess or any of the others. She could understand that. It was a big step to hand over a friend.

Would Julie do it? she asked her now, and her question was answered with a shake of the head. "Probably not."

"Well, there you are."

"Although I would know I should." She paused. "So maybe I would."

Georgia was intrigued by Ian. Although she saw Julie and Angela regularly – they tended to have breakfast at roughly the same time, and met in the kitchen, around the scrubbed-pine table – Ian kept different hours. She knew that he got up early – he went for an early morning run most days – but he very rarely came into the shared kitchen while they were there. As far as she could make out, he slipped out of the flat without having breakfast and often did not return until after nine in the evening.

He was friendly enough on such occasions as Georgia saw him, and he would ask her about her day with apparent interest. He listened as she told him about her lectures and the sometimes heated discussions they had in tutorials. One of her courses involved a module on industrial relations and social change, a subject that had recently become contentious. For the first time in her course, Georgia felt that she was being asked to think about the here and now, rather than to consider dry questions of theory. Plato's *Republic* was all very well, but she found it hard to relate it to anything that was happening in the world about her. But industrial relations, in a time of a miners' strike, was a different matter altogether.

She was making herself a cup of coffee in the kitchen when

he brought up the subject of the strike.

"You said that you were talking about it in a tutorial," he remarked. "What did people think?"

She poured milk into her coffee and took a sip. "It's complicated," she said. "And divisive. There are one or two people who say that Arthur Scargill is going to wreck the economy. They said that we can't carry on spending money to dig for coal that we can buy far more cheaply from Poland or wherever. But there are others who say that people are entitled to protect their jobs, their communities."

Ian was interested. "Can we talk about this in my room?" He nodded down the corridor. "It's a bit of a tip, but you've probably seen worse."

She said, "Of course."

He led the way. There was an etiquette of flat sharing, she reminded herself. You could glance into your flatmates' rooms from outside, but you needed an invitation to go in. Ian had not yet invited her, and even Julie had not seen his room after she had shown it to him on his arrival.

"He's private," Julie had said to Georgia. "Some people are like that. He's not unfriendly – he just keeps to himself."

He had left the door open, and he stepped aside politely to let her enter first. That did not surprise her: his manner was courteous – almost to the point of seeming old-fashioned. She liked that. It was better than the casual rudeness that so many people showed now, fearing that politeness would be seen as middle-class.

"So, this is where you live." She looked about her. He had made the room comfortable enough, in a masculine sort of way. There was a single bed covered with a heavy but slightly threadbare blanket; a couple of easy chairs, one covered with a throw; a desk with a reading light. The light had a shade of dark green glass that cast a glow over the surface of the desk and the nearby wall. There was a bookcase similar to the one in Georgia's own room. She saw that it was already full and that there was a small pile of books stacked beside it. There were posters on the wall: every student room had its posters. One of these was advertising a performance of *Macbeth* at the previous year's Edinburgh Festival. In Japanese.

She turned to him and indicated the poster. "Did you see that?"

He nodded. "It was fantastic. All in Japanese."

She glanced at the poster. Macbeth, in an ornate kimono, glared fiercely at a dagger hovering in the air. "So I see."

"But that didn't matter. The costumes were great and the acting was really physical. You didn't need to know what they were saying."

Georgia told him that she had seen *The Tempest* in Polish once, but had gone to sleep. "I really didn't see the point."

He indicated a chair, and she sat down. He sat on the bed. He kicked off his shoes and tucked his legs underneath him. She watched him. There was something indefinably arresting about this very ordinary act.

"Your room isn't a tip at all," she said. "One pile of books."

He laughed.

"I can tell that you must have been at boarding school," she continued.

A shadow passed over his face. "Is it so obvious?"

She was pleased that she had been right. Her instinct for these things had never let her down. She could tell.

"It's the neatness," she said. "Everything in order – put away."

He shrugged. "Perhaps."

"Those habits are drummed in, aren't they?"

He sighed. "Nobody likes to think that they're the product of a system, do they? But I suppose we all are – in one way or another. We like to imagine that we're all individuals, but I'm not sure about that. Our preferences, our ideas, our way of looking at things: that's all determined by what happens to us."

She met his eyes. She had the feeling there was more that he wanted to say about this, but was waiting to see what her response would be.

"You're right," she said at last. And then added, "But don't you find it a bit . . ." She struggled to find the right word. "A bit *depressing* when you read what the psychologists say about how early it's all settled? In our first seven years, or whatever it is. That's it. The die's cast."

He paused to give her an inquisitive look. "Do you think choice doesn't come into it?"

She told him that she did not. Or at least, not entirely. There was some degree of choice, though – there had to be. "Nothing would matter otherwise. You could do what you wanted, and nothing would ever be your fault."

He inclined his head. "Yes," he said.

She wondered whether he would have more to add, but he was silent. He seemed to be thinking of something; he had become distant.

Then he said, "So, you think we can't help feeling the way we do about things?"

"About what things?"

He shrugged. "About how we feel about other people, for example."

She looked out of the window. It was early evening, but at that time of year the days were short and the sky was dark.

"Are you talking about whether we like particular people? Is that what you mean?"

He hesitated. "Yes – whether we take to somebody. What I wondered is whether that was something we *decided* upon. Or do you just like the people you like because . . . well, because they are the sort of people you happen to like."

Again, he looked at her inquisitively, and she asked him, "Do you mean *types*? Are you talking about our preference for types? As in a liking for blond hair or for people who have dimples in their cheeks. That sort of thing?"

He nodded.

She thought about it. Those tastes, she was sure, were very deeply ingrained. You could not change some preferences, she felt – and she told him this. He agreed, and then went to say, "The miners' strike is a bit like that, I think. People react to it according to their gut instincts. Our political positions are often dictated by what we've been brought up to believe. They're tribal."

"Maybe."

He began to fiddle with a thread from the blanket on his bed. She watched him. If he tugged too hard, she thought, it would unravel. "Angela, for instance."

Georgia frowned. "What about her?"

"She comes from a small mining town. It's one of those places in West Lothian."

"I know," said Georgia.

"Her father may have been a miner," Ian continued. "The odds are that he was."

Georgia could correct him on that. "She told Julie that he was a mechanic, with the bus company. He's too sick to work now."

"She still has strong feelings about the strike. You probably know that. Has she discussed it with you?"

Georgia shook her head. "Not really."

He looked surprised at first, but then he said, "Perhaps she doesn't want to talk to you about it because she thinks you'll be on the other side."

Georgia bristled. "Why would she think that?"

Ian raised an eyebrow. "Perhaps because . . ." He trailed off.

Georgia waited. She had no difficulty imagining that Angela would have concluded she disapproved of the strike, but it was so unfair. She was being judged because of what? Because of the way she spoke? Because she came from where she came from – a long way away from the coalfields and the streets where those noisy, often violent, always impassioned battles were being fought. That was fundamentally unfair. How did Angela know what she felt about the strike? She was sure where she stood: she could see both sides. But they had not asked, and it occurred to her that nobody had asked her for the same reason that Angela had refrained from talking to her about it.

Ian sensed that he had crossed a line. "I'm sorry if you're offended," he said. "I may be wrong about what Angela believes. I was just thinking aloud, really."

"She doesn't know what my views are," said Georgia.

"Of course not," said Ian quickly. And then he added, "She's taking me out there. We're going to her place next Saturday. She said we can go to the local hall and listen to what the men have to say. She said that Mick Johnston will be speaking."

Mick Johnston was a union leader of the old school: uncompromising and unashamedly direct. He had been down the pits himself, and that added to his status among the miners and their supporters. His left-wing views were widely known.

"He'll be fiery," Ian said. "I can't wait to hear him. It'll be like living through history."

He looked at Georgia as if he were assessing an unspoken possibility. Then he said, "Why don't you come with us?"

She was momentarily taken aback. "Me?"

He grinned. Suddenly he was a schoolboy proposing an illicit adventure. "Yes. You'd like to hear Mick, wouldn't you?"

She thought of Angela's invitation to Ian. It sounded a bit like a date, even if a rather unusual one, and she doubted if Angela would welcome an intrusion. And that led her to imagine what Angela might feel about Ian. Georgia looked at him, discreetly, as one might snatch a glance at a handsome stranger in a crowded room. He was attractive in what she might call a quiet way, with his slightly shy, boyish way of looking at you. There was something about his eyes, too, that she had only just noticed. There was a brightness in them, as if he had just discovered something. It was perfectly possible, in fact rather more likely than not, that Angela had noticed all of this and had made her move. *Let's go and hear Mick Johnston.* It was an unusual invitation to a date, but these were unusual times ...

"Well?" he said. "You would, wouldn't you?"

She replied that she was sure it would be interesting. But did he think Angela would mind? It was, after all, her idea and she might not want too much of a crowd.

"Three's hardly a crowd," said Ian.

But it was, thought Georgia – and there was a popular saying to just such an effect. She did not press the point, though, and simply asked, "How do we get there?"

"We take a bus. Easy."

She looked doubtful, but he smiled at her, undeterred. "Honestly, I really think you should. There is something really important going on out there, you know. How will you feel in ten years' time if you think back and realise you had the chance to witness it, and you didn't?"

She did not argue. "All right."

He seemed pleased, and that, in turn, pleased her, because she wanted to engage with him. She had not expected this, but it was happening: this was how it started. She looked at her watch.

He noticed, and invited her to stay. "Would you like to hear some music?"

"I have an essay to finish. It's due tomorrow, and if I don't submit it in time, Dr Dutton won't read it."

His disappointment showed. He was interested in her. Or was he? The feeling she was getting was not the familiar one of male interest – that unambiguous sense of being the object of pursuit. This was different. It occurred to her that he wanted friendship, which was something quite different. Of course, there was every reason for them to be friends: they were flatmates, after all, and the people you shared a flat with tended to become friends, even if not particularly close ones. Was Ian lonely? She decided that he was. She had not seen him with friends, but then she had hardly seen him at all. We may make a major mistake if we assume, as we often do, that the part of another's life that we glimpse is their entire life.

"Will you ask Angela?" she said, as she rose to leave. "Check with her that she doesn't mind?"

"I don't see why she should," Ian said.

Georgia smiled. Could he really be that unaware of female psychology? "Well, maybe not. But sometimes people . . ."

She did not finish the sentence. Ian was giving her a discouraging look.

"There's nothing between Angela and me," he said firmly. "If that's what you're driving at."

She had not intended to reply to this, but it slipped out. "In your view, that is," she said. "She might think differently."

She regretted it immediately. It was quite wrong for her to raise the issue of a relationship between Angela and Ian. He would be entitled to tell her to mind her own business, if he objected, as he might well do. But he did not do this. He got up off the bed and slipped into his shoes. "You need to get that essay written," he said.

As she left his room, she inadvertently brushed against him It was the most delicate of contacts, but she did not think she had imagined it. He appeared not to notice, but for her that brief touch was electric in its effect. She felt that this was a moment that would change everything.

She went back to her room and shut the door. She closed her eyes and allowed herself to imagine what could happen. She saw him before her, arms held out in welcome. She approached him, grateful for his attention, and he embraced her. She put her hands upon his shoulders. In the private theatre of the imagination, she thought, we can pick whatever role we choose for ourselves, confident of our ability to play it with distinction, and in such a way, of course, that the outcome is just as we would want it to be.

She opened her eyes. Nothing had happened between them. He had touched her, or her him, inadvertently, that was all.

And anyway, it was not a good idea to fall for one of your flatmates. That was rule number one in the unwritten but perfectly well-understood list of rules for communal living. And yet, he had made a point of saying that there was nothing between him and Angela, which was another way of telling her that he was available. Rules about non-involvement were all very well, but they were advisory, rather than prescriptive. In an ideal world, don't complicate life by becoming involved with a flatmate, but in the real world, what could you do to stop yourself? These things were beyond our control, and perhaps it was better to accept that and let them happen. People went to university and fell in love. That happened to everybody, or just about everybody. Why should she be any different?

Nine

Spinach is entirely uncontroversial

"IT'S A GREAT PITY," said Mrs Donald, "that deceased people can't have their mail forwarded – like everybody else. I suppose the issue is the forwarding address . . ."

She said this to James, who took a moment or two to realise that it was a joke. He was getting used to the Scottish sense of humour, and to the deadpan way in which remarks like this could be delivered. But understatement and irony both had their challenges, and could take some time to be seen for what they were.

They had met when she called in one morning to collect several letters, mostly bills, which had arrived for her brother. Julie had offered to deliver them, but she had insisted that it would be easy enough to pick them up on her way to her yoga class – *Yoga for Ancients*. "We love the name," she said. "And it's so descriptive. Yoga is an ancient practice, of course."

She came at a time when there would normally have been nobody there to answer the door, as everybody had left for lectures or tutorials. As a postgraduate, James's timetable was lighter and more flexible, and he often spent the morning working in his room. His master's degree would take a year, which he knew would be over before he realised it. He could stay longer if he wished, and convert it into a higher, thesis-based degree, but he thought he would not. There was always a temptation to prolong education in order to put off the day of reckoning when one had to get a job – a real job in the real world. He did not want to do that – nor did he need to. It had always been understood that he would take over the speakers' bureau, which would provide him with a good enough living as long as there continued to be a demand. And the demand showed no sign of abating, and nor did the supply of those willing to speak. There were always out-of-office politicians whom people would turn up to hear – at least for the first few years after they had left office; plus, there were always people like Larry Buckle.

James did not like to think too much about his future. Unlike many of his college friends, he was not ambitious. One friend in particular seemed – to James at least – to be obsessed with success. He had set his sights on law school, and not just any law school: he'd set his sights on Harvard, and was given the place he so desperately wanted. Thereafter the road map was all set out: there would be the clerkship, the job with the Wall Street firm, the years of unremitting toil, then the eventual partnership and everything that went with it. But where, in such a plan, James wondered, was the room for life? Perhaps time could be found after one was forty, although forty, from the perspective of one's early twenties, seemed almost too late. His friend was at Harvard now, and had made a point of saying how happy he was, but James had reflected on the fact that those who stressed their own happiness were usually doing so because happiness, in its perverse way, was eluding them.

On that particular morning, James opened the front door to Mrs Donald, his mind still full of the philosophical paper he had been reading. He had not expected her, as her conversation had been with Julie, who had said nothing about it to her flatmates.

"I," announced Mrs Donald, "am your landlord."

James shifted his weight from foot to foot. Was this an inspection? Did he have to invite her in?

She made her remark about mail for the deceased, and after hesitating briefly, James asked her in. He had spotted the small pile of letters on the hall table, and he handed these over to her, almost apologetically. It seemed poignant that people still wrote to the dead; that there could be entreaties and confidences, perhaps even professions of love and affection, that would go unanswered. There was something ineffably sad about talking to those who would not, or could not, listen. There had been a boy at school who had talked to a small plastic figure of Mickey Mouse that he always carried in his left pocket. James had heard him doing this, but had said nothing because he sensed immediately how lonely the other boy was. And then, without any warning, the boy was suddenly no longer there. Their teacher had been evasive, only muttering something about the boy's family having had to relocate. But there was something more to it, James suspected, and it was not until he was sixteen, two years later, that he learned the father had accidentally driven a golf buggy off a bridge.

Now, as she tucked the letters into the tote bag she had brought with her, Mrs Donald asked James about his course. He told her that it was philosophy, and she looked impressed. "It's something I'd love to study," she said. "But the flesh is weak – I mean, the mind is weak."

"There's nothing abstruse about philosophy," said James.

She smiled. "Except the adjectives one uses to describe it."

"I'm sorry," said James. "What I mean—"

"I understand perfectly," said Mrs Donald. She gave him a sideways look – a look of interest. It impressed her that a young man could devote himself to philosophy when there were so many other, more obvious distractions. Should you *think* at a time when you can still *do*?

She said, "What age was Aristotle?"

He was surprised by the question. "When he wrote his *Ethics*?"

"Yes. Does philosophy have its Mozart – its child prodigy?"

He looked thoughtful. He had never thought about Aristotle's private life, or really about him as a person. "He can't have been young," he said at last. "I don't think you can create a whole philosophical system when you're all that young. Music's different. Music and mathematics: they don't require wisdom."

She asked him what he meant.

"They don't need experience of the world. They don't need the judgement that comes from having seen the way people are."

"I think of Aristotle as being pretty elderly," she said, with a nod. "I imagine him looking like one of those marble busts you see. When I was young – really young, that is – I thought that the ancient Greeks didn't have shoulders or bodies. I thought they just had heads and necks – that they were busts."

This tickled him. "Yes, I can see it. A whole lot of busts mingling with one another in the agora. And nobody would have any legs, or torsos even."

"And the Venus de Milo," she continued, "made me think that there were women without arms. I wondered how they dried themselves after they'd taken a bath."

He laughed. "They would have had attendants. Everybody in the past had attendants, didn't they? I thought that, you know. I thought people had servants until . . . well, until relatively recent times. It never occurred to me to wonder how the people who fulfilled those servant roles got by, having to do everything for themselves."

"That's because the story has always been told by those on top," said Mrs Donald. "Just as history is written by the victors." She closed her bag. "I mustn't keep you. You'll have your work to do." She paused. "You might care to come and see me – if you have the time, that is. I could make you lunch some day and you could tell me about . . . about where you come from in the States."

"New York."

"Oh, my!" She began to move towards the door. "This Friday?"

He said that would suit him well.

"And is there anything you don't eat?"

"Small furry creatures," he said, laughing. "Things that may have a rich inner life. Creatures who provoke anthropomorphism." He looked apologetic. "Well, you did ask."

She smiled. "I do a spinach quiche," she said. "There are no philosophical issues with that, I take it? Spinach is green. That's all."

"Spinach is entirely uncontroversial," he said.

"In that case, twelve thirty on Friday. Julie has my address – she'll tell you how to get there."

James said that he looked forward to it, and then, having shut the door behind her, he returned to his room. He was reading an article extracted from the *Journal of the Royal Society of Philosophy*: "Does the kamikaze pilot *want* to die?" It had been mentioned by one of the lecturers in a tutorial and, being intrigued by the title, he had tracked it down and photocopied it. There are orders of want, said the author of the article. There are things we want in themselves, and things we want in order to achieve some other goal. We may want to visit a tedious relative or a heart-sink friend because we know that is what is expected of us. But at the same time, it would be true to say that we didn't *really* want to spend our precious time on such a visit. So the kamikaze pilot may not want to end his life in that final dive for the deck of an aircraft carrier, but, at the same time, he does not want to miss the target.

He finished reading the article and put it aside. He was not sure that there was much to be gained by such speculation. It was redolent, he felt, of the sort of linguistic philosophy done in Oxford in the 1950s, when people like Freddie Ayer and Elizabeth Anscombe spent their time discussing what people meant by the things they said. He had taken a course in that, and had been bemused: such concern, he felt, was arid and unrewarding. It also missed the real point of philosophy, which was not just to reflect on how we expressed ourselves, but to wrestle with the urgent question of how one might lead a good life. He wanted to do that. He wanted to find meaning in his existence – if that was not asking too much. He wanted to have a better life than people like Larry Buckle or the retired tennis stars who the speakers' bureau sent to speak at country club lunches or annual gala dinners. He wanted something that counted for something. He wanted to do the right thing.

* * *

Mrs Donald lived in a Victorian terraced house with a view of the Pentland Hills. These hills, rising just to the south of Edinburgh, were the beginning of a hinterland of green hillsides and small glens, stretching down into the Border country. In the conservatory, which was tacked on to the house as an Edwardian afterthought, she could sit and watch the constant theatre of the skies to the south – the veils of rain, drifting like gossamer, the scudding clouds coming in from the southwest, the occasional sea-mist, or haar, drifting in from the North Sea less than fifteen miles away. She spent much of her time in this conservatory, with its orchids and gnarled vine stock, working her way through the stack of books on a side table – memoirs, popular psychology – her particular interest – along with the novels of Muriel Spark, the poetry of Norman MacCaig, of Pound, of Eliot. She had been the editor of a cultural quarterly and had worked for seventeen years at UNESCO in Paris. But she still liked looking at the hills and perusing Italian recipes.

There had been a husband, but her marriage had ended after six years, when he succumbed to meningitis. He had been there with her in the morning, discussing a trip to London he was about to undertake for a medical conference – he was an endocrinologist – and then, at four, there had been that telephone call from the Royal Infirmary that had ended, for a time at least, her world. She had not given up her job on her marriage – there had been no children – and she continued in her editorial position. She was free, though, to apply for the position at UNESCO and when, rather to her surprise she was offered the post, she took it.

In Paris she had built up a circle of friends, and for six years had lived with an Armenian translator, Raffi. He was given to moods, and was not an easy man. He had a tendency to invite friends back to their apartment at odd times, and there would be long and heated discussions in Armenian, which she did not understand. When she asked what these conversations were about, he simply shrugged and replied, "Armenia."

"But what aspects of Armenia? I don't like to pry, but I'm interested, you know."

He looked at her mournfully. "I'm afraid you will never understand Armenia."

"Not at this rate, I won't. I simply wondered—"

He shook his head. "There is nothing more to be said."

Eventually she could take it no more. She had tried to accept that he was naturally distant, but had found it impossible. What, she thought, was the point of living with somebody who was barely there for her? "I'm leaving," she said. "I'm going back to Edinburgh."

He had sighed. "I'm not surprised," he said. "I'm a very depressing man."

She looked at him intensely. He had always been honest, and this was another example. One could be *too* honest, she thought. "You could try, you know, Raffi. You could somehow get past your . . . sense of loss. That's what you have, you know – you have a sense of loss."

"I have lost my country. Stolen by Turks and Russians. People say: How is it possible to steal a country? And I reply, It's only too possible. It has happened to us."

She looked away. "I am so sorry," she said. "I understand. But I can't mourn a country I've never known. Perhaps if you'd talked to me about it a bit more—"

He shook his head. "Impossible."

"Then I shall return to Scotland." She paused. "There are people there who believe that Scotland has been stolen too."

He made a gesture of disagreement. "Impossible," he said once more. "Whatever happened in Scotland can be nothing like what happened in Armenia."

Now, in her retirement, she found that she thought little of Paris and her life there. She had a circle of old friends in Edinburgh, and her brother, and after a while it was as if she had never been away. She bought her parents' house from their estate, paying out her brother for his share, then moved in to the bedroom in which she had slept as a child. There was nothing to be ashamed of in that, she thought: people made far too much of getting away from the place where you were born and brought up. And then, much later, they found themselves yearning to return. College towns in America were full of such people, buying houses in the towns where forty years earlier they had been so happy.

She showed James the conservatory.

"I live here, or in the kitchen," she said. "There are eight other rooms, but I rarely use any of them, except for my bedroom, of course. I suppose in a fairer society they would take some of my rooms away and give them to others. I couldn't really complain if they did that."

"Difficult to do, though," said James. "Unless they evicted you altogether."

"Which some might like to do," she said. "And although I would complain bitterly if that happened, I don't think my protests would sound all that convincing. The possession of property, after all, is often a matter of chance. I'm in this house because my parents left it to me – or to me and my brother. I didn't *earn* it."

James looked thoughtful. Once you started to question ownership, he thought, the whole edifice could disintegrate. He had been left the money in Uncle Ed's bank account – he had done nothing to deserve that – it had come to him simply because he happened to be the nephew of the man in whose bank account the funds were lodged. And then there was Larry Buckle's sister – she had got that condo in Boca Raton by being Ed's lover – that was the basis of her claim. In due course, the speakers' bureau would come to him, which would be another unearned benefit.

"You can't unstitch ownership," he said at last. "All that matters is a legal right to whatever it is you're talking about. If you have such a right, then that's that."

She did not agree. "You haven't looked at land ownership in Scotland, have you?" she said. "If you had, you might not think that. Large tracts of land in Scotland were taken from the local people. Certainly, that's the case in the Highlands. Common land was stolen from the clans and became large estates owned by individuals and their families."

James inclined his head. "I don't know much about what happened here."

"And in your own country?" she asked. "Or Australia? *Terra nullius?* I don't think so."

He shrugged. "It's messy." But then he added, "I suppose the issue is how far back you go. How long do ancient claims to land last? People disagree about that – to put it mildly."

Her serious manner gave way to a grin. "I fear that I'm a bit of a socialist. Not blood red, but I certainly don't like inequality. So, when it comes to ownership, I think there should be limits on the extent to which one person can acquire control of people's lives by owning too much. I can't see how anybody can dispute that. It's basic fairness."

"Yes. I probably agree."

"I love the idea of a social contract," Mrs Donald continued. "We agree to obey the law in return for fair treatment – and a share in common goods. As long as the powers that be keep to their side of the bargain, we should accept the prevailing order and behave accordingly. But if we get nothing out of it, we're entitled to resist – to revolt, even. Like the miners. Why should they lie back and let that woman throw them on the scrap heap?"

James hesitated. "It seems a pity—"

Mrs Donald interrupted him. "They have the social contract on their side. Thomas Hobbes."

"There's somebody who brings it all up date. John Rawls. Have you heard of him?"

She shook her head. "I'm rusty on everything. Rawls—"

"I'll get you a copy of his book," said James.

She smiled. "You're very sweet. But I have a large list of books I have to read and I'm not sure I should add another one."

"As you wish. But you'll be able to quote him even if you haven't read him. Just say, 'Hobbes said it all – until John Rawls came along.' People will be very impressed. Nobody will argue with you. I like quoting Proust, but I've read very little of what he had to say."

She laughed. "I read Proust when I was working in Paris. I went through what you might call a Proustian period. I thought it was marvellous. All those characters and Proust's wonderful ability to complicate the moment with memories and associations. I loved it. Then I went off it. I read a Proust biography that made me feel irritated by his . . . well, his louche behaviour. Lying about. All those descriptions of those useless people. I felt that I wanted to cleanse my palate. I wanted to read about ordinary people who don't sit in their room all day and go on and on about the doings of society figures. The Duke of This, the Count of That. I became a bit bored."

She fetched the lunch she had prepared, and they ate it at the small table in the conservatory. She asked him about his undergraduate degree, about what it was like at Dartmouth.

"Did you row? Did you belong to one of those ridiculous – sorry, you probably did – one of those fraternities?"

"They call it the Greek system. Yes, they had it at Dartmouth."

She nodded. He had not answered her question, but perhaps that was what these societies were all about: discretion, if not actual secrecy. "We all have our tribal institutions. I so look forward to the arrival of anthropologists, from New Guinea or maybe the Arctic Circle, to investigate our ways. We've studied other peoples over the years – Pitt-Rivers, Malinowski, and their friends – now they should come and study *us*. Perhaps it's time for *Coming of Age in Morningside*." She paused. "I've read a bit about Margaret Mead. I gather there's a re-evaluation of *Coming of Age in Samoa*. There's a man called Freeman who has published a major debunking. It's just come out. A friend gave it to me. I haven't read it yet because I must say I rather like what she stands for. Liberalism. Freedom for women to decide their own fate. A lot of men are made to feel insecure by that. Their reaction is only to be expected, I suppose. She's going to be subject to much more of that, I suspect."

"But she's died, hasn't she?"

"She has. But that won't make any difference. It's easier to debunk somebody who's dead."

Mrs Donald was interested in the speakers' bureau, and listened in astonishment to the story of Larry Buckle. "I find men like that curiously fascinating," she said. "They're so awful, and yet I can't help but wonder what makes them tick."

"Clockwork," said James. "Guys like that don't have much of an inner life. They simply do the things they're programmed to do. Make money. Meet as many women as possible. Drink. Watch football, or soccer even."

She looked at him. "Whereas you?"

"Me?"

"What drives you? What made you get on a plane and come here to Edinburgh and study philosophy?"

He answered immediately. "I want new experiences. I want to see the world. I want to lead an authentic life . . ." He stopped. "I'm sorry, I sound like some kid who's just read Jean-Paul Sartre and has swallowed the whole existentialist thing. I don't mean to be like that."

"I'm sure you're not," she reassured him.

"Yet they did have a point."

She nodded. "I suppose they did."

There was a short silence. Then she looked at him and said, "Do you mind if I ask you a personal question?"

He shrugged. "I'll answer it if I can."

"Are you single?"

He had not expected this, but he replied quickly. "At the moment."

She nodded. "You could meet somebody, I suppose. Edinburgh's a good place for that. There are plenty of people of your age. All those people in the flat, for example. I can imagine that some of them—"

He laughed. "I'm not sure it's a good idea to fall for your flatmates."

She was still looking at him intently. "They seem nice enough to me – or at least what Julie told me about them the other day. I bumped into her at the supermarket."

"There's nothing wrong with them," he said. "It's just that I don't . . . well, I don't fancy any of them."

She had served them each a glass of white wine. Now she raised her glass to her lips. "I take it you're talking about the girls."

He met her gaze. "Would it make any difference?"

"Not really," she said.

"I was thinking of the women," he said.

"I thought you were." They lapsed into silence. He was surprised by her directness. You did not ask people about their sexuality – you just did not. You might speculate, but you should do that privately. He found himself feeling irritated by her prying. His private affairs were none of her business. And although she owned the flat, what her tenants got up to was no concern of hers. He glanced at her, and then looked away. He wondered if she was some sort of voyeur – unhealthily interested in the emotional lives of others. There were such people – mostly men, he thought, but there would also be women who might also seek vicarious satisfaction in that way. Of course, it was also possible that she was quirky, and did not recognise the limits that normally apply to our conversation – or disinhibited, perhaps, in the way in which some older people were, because they simply do not see any reason to be discreet or allusive.

Then the door that led from the conservatory into the room within was opened. And the mayonnaise assistant entered.

Ten

Innocent, guileless

AS THE YOUNG WOMAN came through the door,
Mrs Donald reached out to take her hand. She held it for
a few moments, as if comforting her, and then dropped it. She
turned to James and said, "You haven't met Lizzie, have you?"

James rose to his feet.

The gesture impressed Mrs Donald, who exclaimed,
"Americans have such perfect manners – still." She directed an
appreciative smile towards James. "See, Lizzie – see how James
leaps to his feet. Young Scotsmen remain firmly seated." She
paused, and looked now at Lizzie, who appeared embarrassed.
"Doesn't it make you feel just a little like Scarlett O'Hara?"

Lizzie glanced at James. They shook hands. "I'm Lizzie," she
said. "I work here."

"Lizzie keeps the whole show on the road," explained Mrs
Donald.

"I clean," said Lizzie, modestly.

Mrs Donald was quick to correct her. "Oh, it's much more
than a cleaning job."

"Well, a bit of polishing," added Lizzie, grinning.

"Shopping, fixing, taking the mail to the post office,
answering the telephone," intoned Mrs Donald. "Girl Friday,
in fact." She paused, to give James an inquisitive look. "I take
it you know about Man Friday?"

He did.

"Because one can't assume anything these days," she continued. "Our shared cultural references may not quite have disappeared, but they're certainly on the endangered list."

James waited. He had learned at their first encounter that Mrs Donald was apt to digress.

"Cultural memory is so important," she continued. "But it has to be refreshed if metaphors are to work. They die, you see."

James glanced at Lizzie. Their eyes met. She smiled hesitantly; an exchange of an unspoken confidence. *Here she goes again* . . .

"For example, plumbing the depths of an issue. We all know what that means, but we don't think of a chunk of lead on a string, let down from the side of a ship. The metaphor has died and become part of the language."

"I suppose so," said James.

"Tell it not in Gath," said Mrs Donald, and gave James a meaningful look.

"Publish it not in the streets of Askelon," said James.

She seemed pleased. "Few people know about Gath." She paused. "There's a lovely children's rhyme, to be recited with a pronounced lisp. *Goliath of Gath, with his helmet of brath, Said to young Thaul: I'm going to thmite you, although you're tho thmall.*"

She turned to Lizzie. "But that's as maybe. You get fed up with me, don't you?"

Lizzie shook her head. "I don't, Alice."

So she's Alice, thought James. She had not given him her first name and he had been uncertain how to address her. "Mrs Donald" seemed formal, but perhaps not unduly so.

He looked at Lizzie. She was attractive. He thought, *I like your face.* The thought was clothed in exactly those words. I shouldn't think in such simple terms, he said to himself. That's what children would say: *I like your face.* But he did. And why? he wondered. Because there was an innocence to it – an unspoiled quality. You could tell cynicism a mile off. You could also see selfishness. And lack of interest; boredom; indifference. There was none of that here in Lizzie.

And he liked the fact that she was tall – not unduly, awkwardly so, but almost as tall as he was. He liked women with long legs. Just as well she can't read my thoughts. Just as well she can't see me looking at her legs, shown off by her tight jeans. Everyone wears denim, he thought. Was there no alternative, even here in Scotland?

"Of course, Lizzie's main job isn't here," Mrs Donald continued. "Lizzie is training to be a chef."

James smiled at Lizzie. She returned the smile, but only briefly. He could see that she did not like being talked about in this way. He did not blame her: he would hate it.

Mrs Donald had more to say. "She works for a terrible man, you know. A bully—"

"He's not too bad," interjected Lizzie. "I've met worse chefs. You know what they can be like. They shout, but they don't really mean it."

Mrs Donald shook her head. "Don't make excuses for him, Lizzie. There's no justification for bullying. These people think they're great artists. Michelangelo or whatever, but they're just cooks." She patted Lizzie's arm. "Not that there's anything wrong with being a cook. It's just that *loud* men, with their bad tempers, need to be stood up to. They shouldn't allow men like that to run kitchens."

"Louis doesn't run the kitchen," said Lizzie. "He's a sous chef. The kitchen's run by Edgar. He's not bad at all. He never shouts."

She looked at James, and decided that she would need to explain. Not everybody understood, she realised. "A sous chef is in charge of a department," she said. "I work in sauces and dressings. I do six months there."

Mrs Donald beamed. "Isn't it marvellous? You can spend *months* in soups, for example, and end up knowing everything you need to know about the subject. I imagine one might even become a soup bore. They must exist. Have you met any soup bores, Lizzie?"

Lizzie laughed. She glanced at her watch. "I'll need to get on with my job," she said. She gestured towards the room behind her. "This job."

"Not her kitchen job," Mrs Donald explained to James. "You see, they don't pay their apprentice chefs all that much, James. Poor Lizzie needs a cleaning job on the side, just to get by."

Lizzie said nothing.

"She should get much more," Mrs Donald went on. "After all, she makes the most delicious mayonnaise. She's the mayonnaise person."

"Mayonnaise assistant," corrected Lizzie. "Louis is technically in charge of mayonnaise."

"Many men are technically in charge of things," said Mrs Donald. "But behind the scenes, it's a woman doing all the work. The economy, the making of mayonnaise – it's the same story wherever you look."

They finished their lunch. James was getting used to Mrs Donald, who had now invited him to call her Alice. "It would not be my first choice of name," she said. "There's something *lost* about the name Alice. Lewis Carroll has a lot to answer for in that respect. The Alice who fell down that rabbit hole spent her time being puzzled, in my view. And then there's that woman who had the distinction of being the mother of Prince Philip. She was Princess Alice of Battenberg. The poor woman spent her time in and out of what used to be called lunatic asylums and then became a nun. What a life she had. She did her best, though, and saved the lives of many Greek Jews during the German occupation. But she was a lost soul, nonetheless."

"Are you lost?" asked James.

She gave him a sideways look. "An interesting question."

He felt emboldened. She had quizzed him, now he could return the compliment.

"No, I'm not lost." She paused. "What I would say is that I'm resigned. A lot of people spend a lot of time looking for a way through life – and never find it. Or at least they don't find the particular way they want. I'm not doing that. I'm not looking for anything."

From within the house, there came the sound of a vacuum cleaner.

"That young woman, for instance," said Mrs Donald.

James said nothing.

"I hope that things go well for her."

"Yes," said James.

Mrs Donald frowned. "She's had a bad start in life – as so many people do. She came from a home completely devoid of books, you know. She told me that herself. Not a single book. Not even the telephone directory."

James shook his head. "Bad."

"Yes, very bad. Imagine a childhood without books." She paused. "Of course, some people never feel the loss. They never start reading – ever. Lizzie isn't like that. She's trying to make up for a pretty mediocre education. That's the state's fault, of course. She's trying. I lend her books – she gets through one a week, even with her work here and in that hotel kitchen of hers. We have long conversations about books."

Mrs Donald was staring through the conservatory glass. In the distance, the Pentlands were dark green. A few clouds, languid white wisps, moved across the sky.

"It would be nice," Mrs Donald said, "if somebody came into her life. I'd love her horizons to be broadened a bit. I'd love her to meet people outside her immediate world – that hotel, that kitchen. She's very intelligent, you know. She just hasn't had the opportunities."

"That's a pity."

"Yes, it is a pity." She paused. "That's why I was keen for her to get a room in that flat."

James frowned. "Your flat?"

"Yes. It would have been nice for her to get to know more people of her own age. Students, for instance. But they gave the room to you instead – which was fair enough. It was their choice."

James bit his lip. He'd had no idea that he had taken the room – so to speak – from Lizzie.

"I'm sorry," he said. "I had no idea."

"Oh, it's not your fault," said Mrs Donald. "These things happen. There's a dreadful shortage of accommodation."

They left the conservatory. Mrs Donald had mentioned a book – Robert Louis Stevenson's book about Edinburgh – that she wanted to lend to James. She went off in search of this, leaving her guest in the entrance hall. He began to study a picture on the wall: a young woman at a desk, with a vase of flowers behind her. In the background, visible through the window, was a range of hills. He thought they were the hills they had seen from the conservatory, but was not sure.

Lizzie came into the room. She was carrying a yellow duster.

James said, "Are the hills in this picture the hills out there?"

She glanced at the painting, then looked at it again. "Possibly. That one looks a bit like the hill behind Carlops."

He felt his heart beating within him.

"Would you like to go out for a drink some time?" he said. He knew nothing about her – whether she had a boyfriend, or whether she would be willing to accept an invitation from somebody she had only met a few minutes earlier; there were any number of reasons why she might say no.

He thought she was not going to reply. But after a short while, she did. "Why not?"

He felt a surge of relief. It had been much easier than he had imagined. "If you give me your number, I could call you."

She nodded. "It would have to be on a night off. I don't work on Sunday and Thursday."

He wrote down her number. "This coming Thursday?"

"Okay."

He collected the book from Mrs Donald, then walked back to the flat, a walk of just over half an hour. It was a warm day for the time of year. A passer-by smiled at him. That happened in Edinburgh, and he had become used to it. You could make eye contact without concern, something that could be difficult in New York. He thought of Lizzie; he was going to see her in a few days, and he knew how it would work out. They would end up going out together. Why not? He was unattached, as she appeared to be too. She was attractive and he was confident that, as he got to know her better, she would be interesting. She also represented something novel: up until now he had only dated college girls. They were all the same, he felt – girls whose families could afford to send them to expensive colleges; girls who had the same air of self-assurance about them – young American womanhood raised with all the certainty that comes with economic security. Now he was with people who were rather different from those with whom he had been familiar. These differences could be subtle, but they were there nonetheless: there were references that were not shared; ways of putting things that were different; there was a whole hinterland of experience and attitudes hidden behind a shared language. There was also an innocence about Lizzie – a guilelessness that he found curiously appealing. It was as if she had stepped out of a world that belonged not to the here and now, but to an altogether earlier time. She was Act One of Cinderella – the young girl who had to work in the kitchen and the scullery while others had all the fun. She had wanted to be part of that other, livelier and more wide-ranging world, and he had taken from her, even if unwittingly, the room that would have enabled her to do that.

Eleven

Angela, Georgia and Ian

ANGELA KNEW ALL THE bus times.
"I used to do this journey every day," she said. "I recognised the same faces – all, like me, going into town and coming out again, day after day."

"Except that you weren't going to be doing it for life," said Georgia.

They were on the bus, passing the turn-off for the airport. A plane climbed sharply into the afternoon air. The bus swayed as the driver allowed another vehicle to pass.

Angela was seated ahead of Ian and Georgia, who occupied seats next to one another. She turned round and gave Georgia a searching look. "Meaning?" she asked.

Georgia said, "Meaning that you're going to get away. You already have."

"Get away from?"

There was a familiar note of resentment in Angela's voice, and this was picked up by Ian.

"She means that you're not going to be living in Armadale all your life," he offered. "Not that everybody wants to get away, I imagine. I'm sure there are people who prefer living in a small town to living in a city. It makes sense."

Angela said, "I could end up going back. It's easier to be in

Edinburgh while I'm at uni, but, who knows, I might go back."

Georgia looked doubtful. She glanced at Ian, as if to ascertain whether he believed this. He remained impassive. Now she said, "We all want to get away, don't we? I definitely do. I don't want to go back to Surrey. It's all too . . ." She broke off, and made a face.

"Comfortable?" asked Ian.

"Yes."

This time it was Angela who looked doubtful. But she said nothing.

"Let's face it," said Ian. "None of us wants to be our parents. We want to be who we are, which is not the same people as them."

Georgia gave him a playful look. "So, what's wrong with where you come from, Ian?"

He looked out of the window. Angela gave Georgia a sharp look from the seat in front. Did she not know that Ian had lost his mother? How could she be so insensitive?

Ian eventually replied. "There's nothing wrong with it. It's a farm. It's a long way from anywhere, though."

"So you don't want to be a farmer?" asked Georgia. "I don't blame you. Getting up at five in the morning to milk cows."

"That's dairy farming," said Ian. "We don't have cows."

"Or cleaning out the barn, then."

Ian corrected her. Georgia was English; she didn't know the words. "Actually, we call it a byre in Scotland."

Angela smiled. "It's not Georgia's fault she's English."

This brought a reaction from Ian. It was a common thing in Scotland to speak disparagingly of the English – a habit that went back centuries. People thought it was all right, but he did not.

"I like English people," he said. "I always have."

Angela was defensive. "I was only joking. I've got nothing against the English."

Ian was not prepared to let it go so readily. "It really gets to me," he said, "when you hear people in Scotland saying they'll support any team playing against England in anything. The English are our neighbours. They're not exactly strangers. Why hope that the Spanish or the French beat them in some football match or other? Surely you should support your neighbour. Isn't that the normal thing to do?"

Angela defended herself. "The English can't complain. They lorded it over everybody for ages. They thought themselves superior to the Scots and the Irish, and everybody really. So should they be surprised if people occasionally object to this? I don't think so." She paused, and then returned even more forcefully to the theme. "Look at what happened in Ireland. The English treated them as a colony –"

Ian interrupted her. "Excuse me, what about the Ulster Plantation? Where did those people come from when they colonised Ulster? I'll tell you – Ayrshire. They were Scots. And they behaved every bit as badly as the English did down in Kerry and Cork and wherever."

"Well, I wasn't going to deny –"

Again, Ian cut her short. "You're probably one of those people, Angela, who claims the British Empire was an English business and nothing to do with the Scots. You know the argument? It was the English who were responsible for Empire – not us. We Scots were an oppressed minority." He paused. "Which is complete rubbish. We Scots were right in there with the imperial project. Big time. We were in the army – generals and so on, as well as ordinary private soldiers.

We were engineers and officials and everybody, really, who kept the Empire going. We have as much blood on our hands as anybody else."

Angela shook her head. "It wasn't working-class Scots who did all that. It was the people who identified with the English. It was a class thing."

Georgia sighed. "Do we have to?" she asked. "Do we have to go over the past all the time. *You* did that, no *you* did it. That sort of thing. Isn't it a bit tired now? An endless blame game?"

Angela did not agree. "You may want to forget the past," she said. "But have you asked yourself why? Is it because you don't like what you see when you look too closely?"

There was a brief silence. Ian rubbed his hands together. "I don't know," he said. "Maybe we should talk about something else. Tell us about Armadale, Angela. What do people do there?"

"They work in coal mines," Angela replied. "Or they try to. Mrs Thatcher has other ideas."

Georgia stared at her. Angela had answered Ian's question, but she felt that the response was directed at her. "I don't like her," she said. "You may not believe it, but I really don't."

"Yes," said Ian. "Don't make assumptions about people, Angela."

Angela stole a reproachful glance at him. Whose side was he on? Did he *like* her? She wanted him to, but not quite as much as she wanted Neil to like her. It upset her that Ian seemed keen to defend Georgia, and indeed had invited Georgia in the first place. She was sensitive to her position in the flat: she was the only one who came from what she would describe as an ordinary background. The rest of them came from privilege of one sort or another, although they were careful not to show it. You could never get over where you came from, no matter how hard you might try to create a new identity for yourself. If you had been brought up in some leafy Surrey suburb, then your attitudes would always be shaped by those beginnings. If you came from a mining town in West Lothian, then that was what you *were* in your essence. You carried that deep within you whatever you might do to distance yourself from those early influences. And no matter how hard you tried to free yourself of prejudice, you would always think the way those with whom you were brought up thought. Were we that trapped by the constraints of home and upbringing? Angela thought we were.

Georgia felt uncomfortable about the atmosphere that seemed to be developing. She felt awkward enough about muscling in on Angela's outing; how much worse it would become if she were to fall out with her while they were, in a sense, her guests.

She tried to sound as placatory as possible. "All I want to do is see at first-hand what's happening. I want to hear what the miners think. I want to find out what people think. Most issues have two sides, after all."

Angela listened to Georgia's words, but said nothing. She wanted to say something about middle-class deprivation tourism; she wanted to say that people in mining towns wanted none of that. Those outside the labour movement were welcome to give their support, but people did not want well-meaning spectators drifting in and out of the dispute. She said nothing, though, because she had invited them to do just that – to come and see. She remained silent for the rest of the short journey to Armadale while Georgia and Ian conducted a sporadic and muted conversation behind her, but she made out little of what was said.

Angela had said that her parents' house was only a couple of blocks away, and they could go there before they went on to the union relief centre where she knew some of the volunteers. "Mick Johnston is speaking at three," she said. "We'll have plenty of time to get to the hall."

"Have you heard him before?" asked Georgia.

Angela nodded. "Once or twice."

"And?"

"He's a powerful speaker," said Angela. "He takes no prisoners."

"I like him," Ian said. "I like people who say what they think. I like people who are not afraid to speak what's on their mind."

"Like Margaret Thatcher?" said Angela, and laughed.

"She does that," said Georgia. "But not everyone likes what's going on in her mind, do they?"

"No," said Ian. "They don't. Particularly in Scotland. She's so . . ." He did not finish.

"English?" asked Georgia.

Ian shrugged. "Well, yes. She represents a certain sort of Englishness that doesn't go down well here."

"You can say that again," said Angela. "Somebody said to me the other day, 'What's the opposite of Margaret Thatcher?' And you know what the answer was? 'Scotland' – that's all."

Ian looked bemused. "No offence, Georgia. It's just that Scotland is different. We believe in –"

"Community," interjected Angela.

Ian hesitated. "Yes, but—"

"But we do," said Angela. "Liberal individualism is going

to end up separating us from people around us. It will be everyone for themselves."

Ian thought about this. "Yes, but what I was going to say was that we also believe in people being independent and working hard to get somewhere in life. That's a Scottish tradition too, remember." He paused. "It's a question of balance, isn't it? You want people to look after themselves and not expect others to do everything for them. But at the same time, we also want those who need help to receive it. That's why we have free medical care."

"I can't believe what happens in America," said Angela. "If you get ill – I mean, seriously ill, with cancer or something – it can bankrupt you. Medical bills can eat up every cent you have. And if you can't afford to pay for treatment, you don't get it."

Georgia said that she found that abhorrent. "Nobody should die from lack of money," she said.

Ian raised a fist in the air. "That's a great thing to say. *Nobody should die from lack of money.* But I'm afraid, that's exactly what a whole lot of people – all over the world – die from: lack of money. Because lack of money means lack of food and lack of housing and a lack of money to buy medicines to treat diseases like malaria – just for instance. There are far too many ways of dying from lack of money."

The bus on which they were travelling turned off the main road.

"We'll be there in five minutes," said Angela.

Georgia looked out of the window. They were passing a corner store, a small newsagent and grocery store at the side of the road. A woman was wheeling a pram past the store's front door. She was smoking, and a small greyish white cloud rose briefly above her, and was then dispelled. Everything had become smaller, it seemed to Georgia: the houses, the road, the trees, the skies.

Ian also gazed out of the window. He was thinking of Neil. Neil had said to him that if he came back in time that evening, he would make spaghetti Bolognese, and they could eat it together. They could go to the pub afterwards, if Ian wanted to. He had a vague arrangement to meet a couple of people from the athletics club in the Golf Tavern. It was nothing definite, but Ian was welcome to come if he wanted to.

Ian said, "Of course I do. That would be great."

"I don't know these guys well, although one of them is from Orkney. And one of them knows a nurse who's from Stromness and who's training in Edinburgh. She might be there."

"I'll be back in time," said Ian. "I'd like to go to the pub."

"Good. I'm sick of work. I've had this project to hand in, and I just want to get out."

"I know how you feel," said Ian. And he thought: *I want to be with you. It doesn't matter where. Anywhere will do.*

The bus took a turning. In the distance, the wheel of a mineshaft was silhouetted, unmoving against the sky. It was such a backdrop that had been used for any number of news reports, accompanied by a soundtrack of angry voices, of shouted slogans.

"We're here," said Angela, rising to stand. The bus was still in motion, and she steadied herself by grasping the top of a neighbouring seat. "Time to go."

There was nothing to surprise them in Angela's home. Her

mother served them tea and sandwiches in a neat parlour at the front of the house. There was a television set, a small bookcase, and a sofa. There was little room for anything else, beyond three easy chairs covered in a green tweedy material. There were two framed photographs on the wall, and a reproduction of a Trossachs scene – a steamer crossing the mirrored surface of Loch Katrine. There was a Wemyss Ware china cat, painted in the way typical of the pottery, with unlikely roses. There was a figure of Tam O'Shanter on his mare, poised in hectic flight. The mare's tail streamed out behind her, although a small piece had broken off the tip. The steamer, the loch, the Burns character, were Scotland. There was tea and a plate of shortbread fingers. They were Scotland too.

Ian looked around him. Was this what lay ahead – this utter ordinariness? He could understand why Angela had been keen to move into Edinburgh. Had he lived here, in this cramped house with its low ceilings and its trinkets, he would want to go – of course he would. And yet this is what most people had to put up with. Most people lived on this scale – some in far more restricted spaces. At least this was clean and cared-for and warm enough.

Georgia watched Angela. She had said nothing about her mother, who had appeared in a faded housecoat. She wondered why people should wear such garments – they were so very unflattering. Were they meant to protect you from the mess of your daily round of cleaning? She smiled at Angela's mother, who returned the smile, even if rather hesitantly. There was an air of defeat about her.

"You must forgive me," she said. "We don't get many visitors. I hope you don't mind shortbread – I would have baked something but my husband, you see, needs to have somebody helping him with one thing or another, and that means that other things remain undone."

"I love shortbread," said Ian.

Angela said, "Shortbread . . ."

"You used to make wonderful shortbread when you were young," Angela's mother said. "You'd bake a whole tray and then I'd take it to the Heart Foundation shop. It was meant to be sold for the cause, but somebody told me that they saw them eating the shortbread themselves – the volunteers who ran the shop, that is."

"They shouldn't have done that," Angela said. "I didn't bake the shortbread for them."

There was a silence.

"An angel passing overhead," said her mother. "That's what they say when there's a sudden silence."

"Angels don't exist, Ma," said Angela.

Her mother turned to face her. "You may say that, sweetie, but what about your name?"

Ian burst out laughing. "Yes, Angela. Why call yourself Angela if you don't believe in angels. A bit inconsistent, don't you think?"

Angela reddened. "Who chooses their own names?" she asked.

"Or the place they're born," Georgia added.

Angela's mother looked at her, uncertain as to whether this was comment on their home.

"It doesn't matter where you're born," she said. "That's not the point."

Angela shifted uncomfortably in her seat. "Georgia didn't mean anything."

Georgia blushed. "I just meant that we all start with what we've got. That's all."

The conversation drifted. Angela's mother talked about what the doctor had said to her about her husband's diet; about how a car had been driven onto the bowling green at the miners' social club – "nothing to do with the strike, just boys joyriding" – and about how a neighbour's cat had had eight kittens in a single litter, and one had gone missing somewhere in the house and could not be found. Angela looked embarrassed, but Ian saw that she smiled from time to time, indulgently; she loves her mother, he thought, in spite of the limitations to her world, the shortbread, the china knick-knacks; of course she loves her mother because that is the most natural thing in the world, our first love. The problem was that some people never get beyond that, and the memory of maternal love crowds out the possibility of new loves. He had lost his mother when he was so young and he sometimes wondered now what it would be like to have an adult relationship with your mother – to be an independent person in a relationship that starts off so unequal and dependent. Perhaps you had to free yourself of that earlier love and let it become a form of disinterested love, like *agape*, that love of humanity that had so inspired him when the school chaplain had first told them about it. He had been sixteen when he first heard about *agape* and had thought it was something to which he should aspire. He wanted to love someone – anyone would do, he thought. *My dearest friend; my dearest friend* . . . But he did not dare, because if he loved someone he was sure that the person he loved would not love him back. And there was a reason for that – it was too deep-seated. He liked those who would not return his feelings in the same way. It was like living in France and wanting to live in Italy. It was that simple. So you had to bottle up your feelings and pretend they did not exist – so that nobody would object. But if you loved people equally, whoever they were, then everyone would agree that you were doing the right thing. And not only that – surely you would be surrounded by a feeling of warmth and resolution. If you hated nobody, then what could touch you? Other people might be malevolent and hateful, but not to you; they could not harm you. "Christian love is like that," the chaplain had said. "It's like a suit of armour. Think of it that way." Was it? he wondered. Did it help the Christians in the Coliseum when the lions were let loose? He had asked that when the chaplain had finished his talk, and had been drawn aside. "There are different sorts of armour, Ian," the chaplain had said. "Some protect the body; some protect the soul." He had looked away, because he always had difficulty in meeting the chaplain's gaze. He thought that was because the chaplain could tell that he did not believe what he wanted him to believe. He did not believe that anybody could rise from the dead, nor turn water into wine, nor do any of those things. He did not imagine that there was a divine being somewhere who was in the slightest bit concerned about what he was thinking, what he was dreaming of. God didn't care if he liked other boys – why should he? Yet others did care; there was a certain symmetry, he thought: someone who did not exist did not mind, and those who did exist, most definitely did mind.

He brought himself back to the room in which they were sitting. Georgia was saying something about the strike. "I'm sorry that people are having to strike," she said. "It must be very hard for towns like this."

Angela looked away. She thought Georgia was trying too

hard. She knew nothing about towns like this; they were nothing to do with her world, and she should not pretend to be what she clearly was not. But her mother did not seem to think that. She said, "That's very good of you. Thank you. It's not affecting us personally too much – my Tom is retired, you see, and he never worked in the mines. But other people . . . yes, they're suffering."

"We're going to the meeting, Ma," said Angela. "At the Town Hall. Mick Johnston."

Her mother pursed her lips. "He's a communist, that man."

At first, this was greeted with silence. Then Angela said, "What do communists actually want? I thought they wanted people to end the exploitation of labour. What's so wrong about that?"

Nobody wanted to speak. Then, turning to her daughter, Angela's mother said, "Communists are ruthless, you see. I know that. Your dad knows that. Remember Joe Stalin."

Angela rolled her eyes. "Mick Johnston isn't Stalin. Nor is Arthur Scargill. They're ordinary working men who want people to have jobs and take home a decent wage." She paused. "And not to have the hearts ripped out of their communities. Does Mrs Thatcher care if people in places like this are told to leave the place they've always lived in to go and look for work in . . . in where? Because there will be plenty of other people looking for work in Manchester or London, or wherever she has in mind. They're nobody there. No roots. No familiar faces. Nothing."

Ian and Georgia exchanged glances. Ian said, "There have been tyrants of every political hue. Hitler and Stalin were the same type, but at different ends of the ideological spectrum."

Angela glanced at her watch. "Well, anyway," she said,

"we're going to have to go. There'll be a crowd – there always is when Mick Johnston speaks."

Her mother sighed. "I can wrap up some shortbread for you, if you like."

Angela started to decline the offer, but Ian had already begun to accept. "That's really kind," he said.

Angela's mother smiled at him. "Young men are always hungry. Not greedy, just hungry."

"How can you tell the difference?" asked Angela.

"I imagine you're missing your own ma's cooking," said her mother.

Angela froze.

"I just love shortbread," said Ian.

They sat in the back row, taking the last of the available seats. Late-comers took up the standing room behind – a group of young men talking among themselves about some football matter, but who stopped when a door at the side opened and three men entered the hall. A handful of people in the front stood up, and this was the signal for others to follow them. Soon the whole room was on its feet. There was applause, and one or two shouts of "Mick, Mick."

The man who introduced the speaker had an array of badges on his lapel, too small to mean anything at any distance. He raised his hands for the audience to quieten.

Now there was complete silence.

The other two men sat down. Mick Johnston stepped forward and took the microphone off its stand. His voice was deep, with a gravelly edge to it. It was a voice that had been roughened by making itself heard over the machinery of the coal face, and by dust.

"Comrades," he began. "I haven't come here to persuade you of anything, because I don't need to do that. I have come here to commend you for what you are doing and for the sacrifices that I know that each and every one of you is making. And you are making those sacrifices because you believe, as I do, that if we do not do this, the industry in which we have all grown up in, and which has provided the raw power needed that keeps this country going will be discarded at the whim of those who believe that the market is all that counts. But I would just point out to anyone who may be in any doubt: the market never made anything. The market never created wealth. The market never built machinery. The market never sat by the hospital bed of a sick bairn. Those things are done by folk like those who live in this town, by folk who do not make off with the profits of the labour of others. The market doesn't care about the people who make up our working communities. The market considers us disposable, if it is convenient for what we produce to be bought at a lower price elsewhere. The market believes that that is perfectly all right; well, that is not all right with us. They say we are a dying industry, but if we are dying, then who is it who's killing us? And I have a message for the government – a message from the coalfields of West Lothian, a message from Fife, a message from Wales and Nottingham and everywhere in Scotland, Wales and England where coal is produced: *we're no deid yet!*"

He was interrupted by applause. A man in front of Angela rose to his feet. He put a fist into the air and then sat down again. Georgia watched. She saw a woman wipe a tear from her eye. Ian saw Angela reach out and put her hand on Georgia's wrist. Georgia seemed taken aback, but only momentarily. She grasped Angela's hand, and Angela whispered something to her that Ian could not hear. He thought Angela might be saying sorry to Georgia, and he was moved by this. You should not be at odds with the people with whom you lived; you should live in peace with them. This was what the strike was all about, he thought: about human community and its protection in the face of great impersonal pressures. The miners were right to object to the depersonalisation of the workplace and the world. We were not simply names on lists of workers; we were people – and people who lived in groups that had meaning, and in places that had associations. Accountants would never understand that, he decided.

Twelve

May 1984

In Sandy Bell's

"FOLK MUSIC," LIZZIE SAID to James. "I wasn't sure you would like it. Some people don't, you know."

"But I do," James said. "Of course I do."

"Good. That's why I chose Sandy Bell's. It's one of those pubs where people can go and take their fiddle out, or sing if they like."

They were walking past the Infirmary, past the entrance to the accident and emergency department. The flashing blue light of an ambulance could be seen on the other side of the wall. It was eight o'clock at night – too early for the main onslaught of the drunks who would come later on in the evening when the crowds spilled out of the pubs and the police picked up the more violent or incapable protagonists in the city's long affair with alcohol. It was their eighth date since that first evening when they had gone out for drink and then dinner in Bell's Diner in Stockbridge. James had taken to Lizzie on their first brief meeting at Mrs Donald's flat, and she to him, even if not until they had seen one another a few more times. They took different things from the relationship: he found her amusing, and she enjoyed their conversation. "You know so much more than I do," she said. "I know hardly anything, and you . . . you've read all those books. What can I say?"

He had been bemused. "Firstly, I don't know all that much. That's one thing that philosophy teaches you when you start to study it: it shows you that you don't know as much as you think you know. Philosophy makes you humble – or it should do."

"But I should feel humble anyway, because I hardly know who David Hume was. I've read a bit about him. He was a philosopher, wasn't he?"

"He was. And a very great one."

She nodded. "Right here? In Edinburgh?"

"Right here. It was at a time known as the Scottish Enlightenment. Everybody sat up and paid attention to what was being said in Scotland, because there were all those pretty impressive thinkers. Hume wasn't the only one. Adam Smith. Dugald Stewart. And others. They were the thinkers of the day."

She looked at the street about her. "And they lived right here, I suppose. On this street, do you think?"

"Probably. Some of them. Now they have monuments and statues in the city, too."

They reached Sandy Bell's with its blue door and its advertisements for whisky. The door was open, and the hubbub of conversation and laughter within could be heard on the street outside. In the background, rising above the voices raised in conversation, could be heard the notes of a fiddle and the accompanying beat of a bodhran drum, like a heartbeat.

James led the way in. He made his way to the bar, where he turned to ask Lizzie what she wanted to drink.

"I should pay," she said. "It's my turn."

He brushed her offer aside. "I want to," he said. "And it's only polite to let me do what I want to do. Remember I'm a visitor."

They both laughed. "You haven't let me pay for anything," Lizzie protested. "That's very old-fashioned, you know. Men used to pay for everything, but that's not what happens today. We're equal, you see. Men, women: we're equal now." She paused. "Isn't that the same in America?"

James grinned. "We're *very* equal," he said. "But that doesn't mean I can't pay when I'm in a position to do so."

The funds from his uncle were going far further than he had imagined they would, and he had no need to economise. It was a pleasant financial surprise: this city was so inexpensive when compared with New York. There were some costlier places, but they were mostly on the other side of town and he had yet to explore them. This part of the city, the university town, was well catered for by ordinary cafés and bars that charged ordinary prices.

He ordered drinks and then, with Lizzie at his side, made his way to a couple of spare seats at the end of the room.

She said, "Who do you listen to?"

"The person everyone listens to. Bob Dylan. I like him."

She smiled. "Of course. Who doesn't? Who else?"

He hesitated. He did not want to sound banal. "Simon and Garfunkel. I like them. Okay, they sound very commercial, and I suppose they are. But some of their songs are just so . . . well, they make me feel really sad. That one about going off on a bus to look for America. That makes me want to cry, I suppose. Music can do that, can't it?"

"Of course."

"And there's nothing wrong with 'The Sound of Silence'. We've all heard it a thousand times, but so what?"

Lizzie looked thoughtful. "Why was darkness his old friend, though? I used to think about that line. What does it mean?"

He shrugged. "That he feels more comfortable in the darkness. That it hides the things he finds painful. It's a position. Any of us might want to shut out those things we find distressing. That's why we seek distraction. It's why we like reading or watching films. You've heard of T. S. Eliot?"

She looked at him reproachfully, and he apologised. He realised he had been tactless. "Sorry. Plenty of people haven't." He felt he needed to explain. "Remember, I'm a stranger here: I don't know what people over here know or don't know. Some of my fellow Americans know nothing at all. You'd be surprised." He sighed. "Nothing."

"We have people like that. Everywhere has them."

"Not as ignorant as some of ours. I met somebody once who had never heard of the Netherlands. That was in New York, which is one of the smarter places. If they don't know something like that in New York, then imagine what they don't know down in Little Rock."

"Where's that? You see, I didn't know that."

"It's in Arkansas, which is down south a bit – not quite Louisiana, but next door, more or less. Anyway, T. S. Eliot—"

"What about him?"

"He said that humankind cannot bear much reality. Or words to that effect."

"And do you think he's right?" asked Lizzie.

"Oh yes. Reality's grim – most of the time. Reality is what people have to put up with when they don't have any other choice."

A man who had been sitting on a stool at the end of the bar now stood up. He was a tall and rather shambolic figure. He was wearing a grey tweed hat, perched on the top of his head. He had gentle, playful eyes – eyes that invited you to enter into a conversation, or listen to a snatch of song. He cleared his throat, and people turned to look at him. Lizzie whispered, "Do you know who that is?"

James looked at her. He noticed that she had two small dimples, one on either cheek. He must have seen these before, but not made anything of them. Now he realised that he loved them. And he loved her – that was what he decided he now felt. He wanted to be with her. He thought about her at odd moments. He loved the idea that she worked in a hotel kitchen, and that she made mayonnaise. He loved the way she walked. He loved the curve of her hips. He loved everything about her, and he thought that tonight he would invite her back to the flat and ask her to stay. He wanted to wake up with her beside him. He wanted the morning to dawn with her head on the pillow beside him. He wanted that so very badly.

Now she told him who was the man who had taken to his feet. "That's Hamish Henderson. Everybody knows him in folk circles. He's a collector of folklore. He discovered Jeannie Robertson."

"I'm afraid I don't know who that is. Jeannie Robertson?"

"She was a very famous singer," she said. "She was a member of a traveller family. Her people had been musicians for generations."

James looked puzzled. "Traveller?"

Lizzie explained. "You would probably use the word *gypsy*. We don't use that any more. They were called *tinkers* in Scotland. Again, people say that's insulting. Traveller is better – because that's what they do."

"And they sing?"

"Traditionally, yes. She knew a vast number of songs, and Hamish recorded her singing them."

James looked across the bar. A hush fell over the crowd as the tall man began to sing. It was a soft voice, but each word was carefully articulated and carried well.

"That's 'Freedom Come All Ye'," whispered Lizzie. "It's one of his most famous songs. It's all about—"

"Freedom?"

"Yes. Brotherhood too. Brotherhood is something that Scotland has always prided itself on. There's a famous poem by Robert Burns which makes that point. *That man to man, the whole world o'er, shall brithers be . . .*"

He looked at her. He had had girlfriends before this, but he had never talked to any of them about these things. He felt like a traveller in a foreign land who suddenly comes across a place where they speak his language.

He listened to the song. "I'm not sure I understand," he said to her.

"That's because it's in Scots."

"I see."

"But you get the general message?"

He nodded. "I think I do."

They spent almost two hours in the bar, eking out their drinks. They talked about music. They talked about her job, and the personalities of the kitchen. "The people I work with are all right," she said, and then qualified her remark with, "Most of them. But we have more than our fair share of misfits. They gravitate to kitchens. Big egos. Tempers.

Drinkers. I see all of them."

"While you keep yourself busy making sauces?"

"And mayonnaise. Don't forget the mayonnaise."

He said that he could never forget the mayonnaise. She was the first mayonnaise maker he had ever met, although there must be others. "Are they all as nice as you?" he asked.

He did not mean to embarrass her, but she blushed, and looked away.

"One day," he said, "will you teach me to make mayonnaise?"

She looked back. "If you really want to learn."

He nodded. "I'd like to."

"Then I will."

He finished his drink. "It's ten o'clock," he said. "Shall we go?"

They walked together back to the flat. There was nobody about, as far as he could make out. "They often don't come back until later," he said.

"I'd love to live with a whole lot of people like this," she said. "There would always be somebody to talk to. To have a coffee with. Just to have people around, if you know what I mean."

He caught his breath. "Let's go to my room," he said.

He closed the door behind him. He did not reach for a switch, but there was still a certain amount of light from the open window. The sky was barely dark, the moon a great hanging night-light.

He took her hand. "I've had an idea."

She shivered.

"Are you cold?"

"No," she said. "I'm not cold. What idea?"

"Live with me."

She was silent for a few moments. He wondered whether he

had said the wrong thing. Had he been too direct? But then she said, "Where?"

"Here."

"But you said that what's her name—"

"Julie."

"Yes. You said that Julie had said there could only be six people. You told me she said that when we talked about how you had got the room before I came to see if it was still free. Remember?"

He gripped her hand more tightly. "I know what Julie said. But then, nobody need know."

"What?"

He lowered his voice. Nobody could hear them, as his room was at the end of a corridor. Now he spoke in the way of somebody discussing a military secret.

"You could easily live here without anybody knowing. We don't go into other people's rooms except by invitation – if we want to see people, we go to the kitchen. From ten each morning, there's usually nobody here at all except me. You told me that you usually start work at eleven. And you don't get back till late. So it wouldn't be hard to keep out of people's way."

She laughed. "Are you serious?"

"Yes. Completely serious." He paused. "And it would make no difference to any of the others. I pay rent for this room. I pay my share of the bills. It wouldn't be as if we were taking anything from anybody."

She thought about alternatives. She wanted to live with him, it was true – she was sure of her feelings in that regard. It would be possible. For them to live together in her flat – she thought her flatmate would not object, but it was cramped and barely large enough for two, let alone three. It was also dark, and a bit depressing, and there were neighbours whose strident arguments – and passionate make-ups – could be heard through the walls. Even if some garrets were romantic, hers was not one of them. This was her chance to get away from all that. It may not last, but she did not particularly mind impermanence.

"What if I wanted a bath? What about the bathroom?"

He replied that there were two bathrooms. The one in his corridor was used only by him and the two other men. "We call it the boys' bathroom. You could slip in and out of that and nobody would notice."

She hesitated. "I don't know," she said. "It's a crazy idea, but—"

"But what?"

She swallowed hard. "I don't know if I feel up to it. I thought I'd like to live with the sort of people you're sharing with, but they're all so much more . . . well, they're all students and I'm nothing more than a person who works in a hotel kitchen."

He gripped her hand. "Nonsense. You're as smart as they are – easily."

"I don't think so."

"Well, I do."

She moved closer to him. She kissed him gently, on the cheek. "All right."

Her acceptance came as a surprise. He had imagined that he would have to do more persuading, and even then, he was not sure that she would agree to what he proposed. It sounded almost absurd – the sort of thing that would be considered only to be laughed off.

She said, "If you want me to, I will."

His voice was excited. "I do. Starting right now."

"Tonight? You mean tonight?"

"Yes. You can get your things tomorrow."

She realised he did not mean that she should saunter in openly, carrying a suitcase.

"Discreetly," he added.

He wrapped his arms around her. She closed her eyes. She thought: is this happening to me? Does he really like me, of all people, when there are so many more interesting girls in this city? He comes from New York. He's got money. He shares with these students, and he's asking me to live with him, in secret, and I have said that I will, because nothing else as exciting as this has ever happened to me, and maybe it really is my turn now.

Thirteen

Just a bunch of kids

WHEN NEIL MENTIONED TO Angela that it was his birthday the following day, she asked whether she could make him dinner.

"You're probably going out," she said. "But if you aren't, I could make moussaka for you. I'm not a particularly good cook, but I'm proud of my moussaka." She paused. "Or something else. Chicken Kiev? Do you like chicken?"

"I love moussaka. And that's really kind of you."

"So you weren't going to do anything?"

He shook his head. "One of the guys in my year said he was going to the pub, but I'm happy to opt out of that. Moussaka's much better."

Angela showed her pleasure. "And ice cream for afterwards?"

Neil said that he liked ice cream almost as much as moussaka. He would buy a bottle of wine. "Something Algerian?"

She looked uncertain.

"Not really," he said. "Italian, I think. As long as you're okay with that."

They sat down in the kitchen at seven the following day. Julie had just finished cooking something for herself, and was now washing up. She was going to a concert at the Queen's Hall, and was in a hurry. She gave Neil a kiss on the cheek for his birthday and left.

* * *

"My father," said Neil, "told me once that he had only ever designed one building that he was really proud of. One building – *one* – in thirty years as an architect. Don't you think that's sad?"

Angela looked down at her plate. "Is the moussaka okay?" she asked.

"Fabulous. But just think of that – one building out of hundreds, I suppose."

She looked thoughtful. "Most people have jobs that involve a lot of the same old same old. Architects are probably no different. My father did the same thing year after year. I don't think there was any variety."

"Yes, but *one* building in all that time," he persisted.

She asked him what it was, and he told her that it was a small hotel. "It wasn't anywhere in Orkney – he got the commission from a friend he'd been at university with. This guy wanted to build a hotel in Pitlochry. He asked my father to design it. He said, 'You do whatever you want.' Apparently, clients don't say that to architects very often."

"So, what was it like? Did you ever see it?"

Neil nodded. "He took me there last year. He was very keen for me to see it."

She asked what it was like.

"I really liked it. It was a hotel, of course, and you know what hotels are usually like. But this was different. "

She said that it would have been awkward had he not liked it.

"Very," he agreed.

"Would you have told the truth, or would you have pretended to like it?"

He thought for a few moments. "I don't think that you have to tell the truth if it involves hurting somebody's feelings and –"

Angela interrupted him. "But then you would have to mislead people – sometimes badly. A friend comes to you and says, does this dress suit me, and if you look at her and think, *It doesn't go at all with your colouring*, then you don't say, *Oh, it's great*. You don't. You think of a way of getting the message across tactfully. You say, *It's not bad but I think a different shade of pink would work better with your hair* . . . And you say, pretty quickly, *Not that there's anything wrong with pink*. But your friend has incredible flame-red hair, I mean really the clash is extraordinary, but you still don't say it."

He did not argue the point. "I didn't have to make anything up. I told my father I thought his hotel was beautiful. I said it was the most beautiful hotel I'd ever seen. And he was really pleased. I could see that. No surprise, I suppose. If somebody tells you the hotel you designed is really beautiful, of course you're going to be pleased."

She asked why it was so beautiful.

He replied with a question of his own. "How do you define beauty?"

She thought, impermissibly, *You*.

And so she looked away. If she held his gaze, she would end up saying it, and she was sure that would embarrass him. Women tended to enjoy compliments of that sort, but she was not certain that men did. Perhaps vain men did – those narcissistic types who were always glancing at their reflection in the mirror or a shop window, who had their eyebrows trimmed when they went to the barber. Her cousin, Billy, had objected to that she remembered with a smile. "There was this barber, you see, who asked me whether I wanted him to do something to my eyebrows. Eyebrows? I thought, *Mind your own business, pal.*" Neil, she thought, was indifferent to his eyebrows, and probably did not care too much about his appearance. There were some who did not have to bother about the angle from which they were looked at, having nothing to hide. That was natural beauty.

"So," prompted Neil. "What is beauty?"

"Something that strikes us as being . . ." She struggled to find the word.

He helped her. "Harmonious? Is that it?"

"Yes, along those lines. Julie was talking about something like that the other day. You weren't in. I was here with Julie and Georgia, and Julie told us about a lecture she'd gone to on aesthetics."

Neil smiled. "So that's what women talk about among themselves."

"Sometimes. What do you think we talk about, anyway? Clothes?"

He assured her he would never suggest that.

"And men?" she said. "What do *you* think *we* think you talk about?"

He had a ready answer. "You think we talk about sport. Football and so on. And cars. You think we chat about that sort of thing."

"Well, don't you?"

Neil sighed. "Sometimes. But it depends on the men. I never talk about football. I find football tedious. You know which way it's going to end. Somebody's going to kick the ball into the goal and everybody will jump about and shout their heads off. Frankly, that bores me."

"Which leaves cars."

He said that he did not mind cars. "But there's not all that much you can say about them – unless you get really technical. And I've never had a conversation with anyone about acceleration or suspension or torque."

"Perhaps you're missing something."

He shook his head. "I don't think so."

She toyed with a forkful of moussaka. "Are you sure this is okay?"

"I told you," he replied. "It's really good."

She took a sip of wine. He had spent slightly more than he had intended, and had drawn her attention to the label. "This is Bordeaux, you see. Look. Saint-Estèphe. We went there once, when I was fourteen. My dad likes wine. He thinks he knows a lot about it, but I suspect he doesn't really. I once poured him a glass of Italian wine – it was dirt cheap – and he said, 'This is a very nice claret.'"

She thought he might just have been being polite. "Perhaps he knew straight away, but didn't want to hurt your feelings."

"I don't think so. My dad is fairly direct. If he doesn't like something, he says so. He's lost clients that way. They tell him what they have in mind, and he says that it's a rubbish idea. They get offended and go to another architect. Or should I say, the other architect, as there is only one other in Orkney."

Now she tasted the wine again and said, "Portuguese."

He laughed. "Wrongly labelled? Maybe."

She wanted to know more about the hotel, the one which had started their conversation about beauty. Neil was easy to talk to – one topic led on to another quite naturally. She could talk to him for hours, she thought. It would be like a stream that seems to be going nowhere in particular, but just continues to flow.

"That hotel," she said. "The one your father designed, and which you said you liked so much – what was so special about it?"

He looked thoughtful. "He followed a language."

She looked puzzled. "Sorry, I don't quite . . ."

"Buildings talk a language, you see. They have a grammar that you can see at work in the way the various elements hang together." He paused. "Am I making sense?"

She understood what this was about. "Back to harmony," she said.

"Yes, but there's more to it than that. There was a professor of architecture called Christopher Alexander. He was at Berkeley, in California, and he wrote a book that I really love. It was all about the principles of humane architecture. That's the opposite of brutalist architecture. Brutalist architecture says *wham!* It's in your face, or it's a kick in the solar plexus. No concession to subtlety or ambivalence. Nothing. Flat surfaces. No relief. Impersonal. No ornament."

She said she knew what he was talking about. There were brutalist flats not far from where she had been brought up. The people who lived in them mostly hated them. There was nothing for the soul in such buildings.

Neil agreed. "No connection. No sense of neighbourhood."

"And people are trapped if the lifts don't work."

He winced. "The planners who commission such buildings never live in them, do they?"

She looked thoughtful. "Just like the people who close mines down – they don't live in mining villages."

He looked up. There was a note in her voice that reminded him this was a painful subject. "I'm sorry about the strike. I know you come from West Lothian. I know there are mines there."

He wondered whether to say more, but decided against it. He sympathised with the miners and had been dismayed by the pictures he had seen in the papers of the fights on the picket lines. He understood that they were trying to preserve a way of life, but at the same time he saw a certain hopelessness in their cause. Deindustrialisation was a fact of life. If there was less need for coal, then was there any point in continuing to mine it? He sensed that this was not the time to raise that doubt.

He had more to say about the hotel. "I loved it because it embodied so many of the principles that Christopher Alexander talks about. All the walls had recesses in them – places where there would be shadows breaking up the surface. There was a courtyard – and Christopher Alexander says that a courtyard is the space in which people feel most comfortable. Did you know that? We are at ease in a courtyard because we feel secure. Nobody can surprise us by creeping up behind us. It's that simple."

"I suppose so. I hadn't thought about that." She paused, before continuing, "I like courtyards too. I'd like to live in a courtyard."

"The worst place to live," Neil said, "is in a house that is in a long street of houses. People who live in places like that tend not to know their neighbours. It's just the way we are. We can't relate to people when we're in a really long line like that. It's the same as at a bar. When you see those pictures of the typical American bar, there are people sitting shoulder to shoulder not talking to one another – because they are all facing the same direction. Nobody is face-to-face. There's a picture called *Nighthawks*. We looked at in our urban design course. It's by an American realist artist called Edward Hopper. He painted loneliness. This picture shows a diner at night with people not relating to one another. That's what you get, you see."

"I think I know it."

"His paintings have people in them," Neil continued. "But they aren't talking to one another. They're all very lonely."

They was a silence, broken at last when Angela said, "I really like living in this flat, you know. I really like sharing with others. We seem to get on very well, don't you think?"

He agreed. "It's a good mix. And we're lucky that this flat is so large. I think it makes a difference having six people. Sometimes, if there are three or four sharing, you get issues. Perhaps it becomes too intense – I don't know."

Angela hesitated. "I wasn't sure about Georgia, to tell the truth. When I first met her, I thought that she was typical of some of those people you get in George Square – people from privileged backgrounds who have had it all handed to them on a plate. A lot of them think they're a cut above the rest of us. Their sense of superiority grates with me, I'm afraid. They condescend."

"She isn't like that, though," said Neil. "Georgia has no airs. She might come from a well-off background, but that doesn't mean she's a snob, or anything like that."

"No," said Angela. "I found that out when I got to know her a bit better. She came out to Armadale with Ian the other day. I could tell she was moved by what she saw. We went to hear Mick Johnston. I could tell she understood what he was saying. It was obvious. I felt a bit bad, actually, that I had written her off before."

"Well, we can all do that. We can all misjudge people." He paused. "You went with Ian?"

"Yes. The three of us. You weren't around. Otherwise, I would have asked you."

He assured her that he did not mind. "We can't live in one another's pockets." He looked at her enquiringly. "Did Ian enjoy it?"

He did, she said. He had been quiet in the bus on the way back, as if he was weighing up what he had seen and heard.

"He thinks a lot," said Neil. "And he's not one of these people who goes on and on. He chooses his words."

"I like him," said Angela.

She waited, as if expecting him to concur. Or differ, perhaps?

"I like him too," said Neil. He looked at her, and she realised he had something to add.

"But?" she asked.

"But I'm not sure I can be the friend he would like me to be."

She was not sure she understood. "You're on different wavelengths?" she asked.

He shook his head. "Not that. It's just that there are some people who expect a bit more of their friends – that's all. It's not a big point."

It suddenly occurred to her that she knew what he was saying.

"Do you feel sorry for Ian?" she asked.

The question surprised him. "A bit, perhaps. There's a sadness there, don't you think. There's something wistful."

From down the corridor, they heard a sudden burst of

laughter. It was short, and it was almost immediately stifled. They looked at one another.

"Was that James?" she asked.

Neil shrugged. "It came from his room, I think."

She lowered her voice. "Has he got a visitor?"

"I don't know," he said. "We don't see much of him, do we?"

"Perhaps he's reading something amusing and it made him laugh," said Angela.

"Could be."

"Do you think he likes us?" asked Angela. "I mean, there he is, a postgraduate, and we're just a bunch of kids."

"He's only two years older than most of us," Neil pointed out. "That isn't so much."

There was another noise from the end of the corridor. This time, it sounded like something hitting the floor.

"Now he's throwing his shoes about," whispered Neil. "Maybe he's reading something he disagrees with."

They both laughed.

"Odd," said Angela, looking slightly regretful. "Still, none of our business."

Fourteen

Landscape with the Fall of Icarus

JULIE LIKED TO ARRIVE early for lectures, even one like this, which started at five past nine. The five minutes was an academic tradition – a concession for the benefit of latecomers. She never availed herself of that, and was usually in her chosen seat, halfway up the lecture theatre, a good ten minutes before anybody else, a result, she admitted, of having been brought up in a household where meals were served at precise times and nobody lingered in bed in the morning. A friend once laughed at what she called her obsessive punctuality, but she was cheerfully immune to her criticism. "There's nothing wrong with a mild degree of OCD," she retorted, adding, with a smile, "And by the way, your collar's not quite straight."

People tended to sit in the same seats at lectures, often with friends with whom they might conduct *sotto voce* conversations when they lost interest in what the lecturer was saying. Julie did not do this; although she knew most of her fellow students – there were slightly over a hundred of them on her course – she did not want to be distracted during the lecture. Now, sitting back in her seat, she paged through the notes she had taken the previous day. They were doing a segment of the course in which they looked at one particular painting in detail, chosen simply because it appealed to the lecturer. Dr Brock, who was running the course, was fond of narrative painting, with the result that he often chose subjects drawn from classical mythology. The previous day it had been a portrayal by a seventeenth-century neo-classical painter of the finding of the infant Paris. "Had that agreeable old goatherd not stumbled upon him," he observed, "the history of the classical world would have been quite different. There would have been no Trojan War, because Paris would not have abducted Helen, and the Greek fleet would never have set sail."

Julie wrote in her notes: "Brock suggests a category of counter-factual painting, expressing the world we would *like* to exist if things had been a little bit different." She had jotted down a few examples, and then written, "But the point about mythical subjects is that they never existed anyway. Why speculate about things that had never happened in the first place and bore no relation to reality anyway? The imagination need not be constrained by historical laws." Now, reading her notes again, she realised that she was not sure what she meant. She pencilled in a large question mark in the margin, and wrote, "Does this make sense?"

She looked up. More members of the class had arrived and were filling up the front rows of the theatre. In one of the seats immediately in front of her a young man she recognised but had never spoken to sat down. As he opened a large notebook and placed it on the desk in front of him, Julie ran her eyes over the jacket he was wearing. It was oatmeal in colour and was frayed at the cuffs. She noticed that there was a line of grease around the collar, and that the garment had about it the smell of stale sweat. It was the smell of an unwashed garment – that unmistakeable slightly rancid smell that was indistinguishable from the smell of an unwashed body. She moved back in her seat, instinctively, just as the young man turned slightly. He was still looking ahead, but she saw him now in profile and noticed his slightly retroussé nose and his untidy rug of hair. She saw one of his hands on the notebook, the nails bitten to the quick. She held her breath, momentarily disgusted. She wondered whether others noticed this – it was her sense of smell again, and she might be the only one. She was not always comfortable being able to tell who had washed and who had not.

She looked about her. In the seats in front of the young man, there were several members of the class whom she knew quite well. One of them turned and smiled at her, paying no attention to the young man. There was no wrinkling of the nose; no sign of distaste.

Dr Brock entered from a door behind the lecture podium. He was a man in his late thirties, with an aquiline nose and a patrician manner. He spoke in the careless drawl of an English public school – he had been at Harrow – overlaid with a layer of Oxford precision. He had been a research fellow at Christ Church, but had taken the post in Edinburgh, some said, because of a minor scandal involving a female undergraduate. If anything, that gave him a romantic rather than a grubby air. She had been Persian, people said, and was some relation of the Shah. Dr Brock lived in a New Town flat and gave good parties. His book on Modernism was widely quoted in the footnotes of other scholars. He had been a croquet player in Oxford, and had on two occasions played for England.

Now Dr Brock stood at the podium and brought up on the screen behind him a slide picture of the painting they were to discuss. Julie looked at it. It was a familiar image, and she had seen it many times before, although she had not paid it any particular attention.

Dr Brock began his lecture with a brief recital of facts. "Brueghel," he said. "Pieter Breughel, a member of a family that gave us several painters. This Pieter is Brueghel the Elder, who also painted a memorable depiction of the Tower of Babel, which I imagine most of you will know." He pointed to the screen, to the wide, Colosseum-like building that filled almost the entire canvas. "This painting, executed about 1560, only reappeared in public view in the 1930s, when it was bought by a Dutch collector, who kept it, we are told, above a stove on which he used to fry sausages. Great works of art have survived even more significant dangers, although their close shaves with damage or destruction always give us a frisson of retrospective anxiety."

The young man sitting in front of Julie laughed. He turned in his seat, as if to share the joke. She caught his eye, and smiled weakly. She wrote in her notes: *Brock says don't keep Brueghels above frying pans.* And crossed it out, feeling that it was childish. And yet she knew that she would remember the provenance of that painting because of the anecdote.

Dr Brock continued. "But enough of *Babel*, what I should like to talk about this morning is this painting here – also by the elder Brueghel, probably painted during the 1550s."

The picture on the screen changed, and once again Julie recognised the image that came up. A ploughman, his back half-turned to the painter, holds his plough as it describes curved lines in the soil; to his right, the ground falls sharply to a shoreline grazed by sheep, and to a green sea, with islands. The ploughman treads lightly on the freshly cut earth – it seems that he is about to dance. The horse looks resigned, at least in its posture – we cannot see much of its head.

In the sea an elegant, three-masted ship, with only one sail unfurled, sails past a headland. The ship is in motion, but only just. Behind it is the main point of the picture, even if it occupies only a tiny part of the canvas: a naked, human leg, pointing up at the sky, upright above the surface, attached to a figure we do not see, as it has already splashed into the water.

"You will see," said Dr Brock, "that there is a human leg disappearing beneath the surface of the sea, but still visible. Something has happened: somebody has dived down into the sea from above. That, of course, is Icarus, the son of Daedalus. He and his father have made wings for themselves to return home, but Icarus ignores his father's advice about not flying too high. The wax that holds his feathers in place melts, and the boy falls to his death. If a painting sets out to underline a moral, it is usually pretty obvious: don't fly too close to the sun. We all might heed that message, even if we have no immediate plans to make ourselves wings."

The young man in front of Julie laughed quietly. Suddenly she felt sorry for him. She suspected that he might like to have friends about him to share his amusement. Things are funnier in company. But if he wanted friends, she thought, he would have to pay more attention to personal hygiene. Could she tell him that? It was said to be the one thing you couldn't say, even to your best friend. You cannot tell people they smell. You simply can't.

Dr Brock said, "Look at the leg. You will observe that Brueghel seems to ignore the rules of perspective here: the leg is far bigger than it should be when looked at against the size of the ship, which is only a short distance away. And I am not sure that the foreground – the ploughman and his horse – are in proportion to the middle ground, the shore and the ship. Yet the rules of perspective are there to be broken if otherwise an important element in the picture would be too small to see.

"But these are technicalities. The story of Icarus is only of moderate interest. It is a story that we all know very well, which means that a painting that simply tells it without adding much else is not going to be very memorable. This painting could be banal, but it is far from that, which makes us ask whether there is something else that the artist wants to say to us. This is the second degree meaning – the message beyond the narrative.

"And it is W. H. Auden who brings that to our attention in this case, in an ekphrastic poem that he wrote in December 1938. An ekphrastic poem is one that is inspired by another work of art – in this case, it is about a painting. 'Musée des Beaux Arts' was written by Auden after he saw the painting in Brussels. Note the date. Europe was on the brink of war. The unspeakable was about to happen."

The normal sounds of a lecture theatre – the faint rustle of papers, human sounds such as the clearing of throats – these all stopped. The silence, it seemed to Julie, was complete. She stared at the image on the screen – at the lithe ploughman in his inappropriate doublet; at the single human leg; at the sky, which was white and grey; at the green of the sea and of the land. She waited.

"Auden starts his poem with a bold generalisation. If you write a poem, I always think, begin it with a strong line that proposes something. *About suffering, they were never wrong.* That's his first line. Who was never wrong? He goes on: *The Old Masters; how well they understood/ Its human position . . .*

"And that position is in the middle of ordinary things that

are happening around it. Suffering, he says, takes place when people are leading their ordinary daily lives, getting on with their business. So, in this picture, Auden says, the ploughman may have heard the boy's cry as he fell from the sky, but for him it was 'not an important failure'. And the 'expensive, delicate ship' may have seen something amazing, but has somewhere to get to and sails calmly on.

"And there you have it: a profound and shocking message. Suffering is all about us. It happens under our noses, but we have somewhere to get to and we sail calmly on."

He stopped. The silence persisted. Julie held her breath.

She leaned forward slightly, and reached out to touch the young man in front of her on the shoulder – a gentle touch, a passing tap. He looked round, surprised.

"Hi," she said, smiling at him.

He looked puzzled.

"Just saying hello," she said.

He grinned, and turned back to his notebook.

"Just think about it," said Dr Brock.

After the lecture, Julie had a couple of hours to kill before a tutorial at twelve. There was an essay to write, and she should have gone to the library to work on that, but she felt unsettled. It was a fine morning, and the sky above the city was clear of cloud. If she were to walk down to the National Gallery of Scotland, that would take twenty minutes or so. She could then spend an hour looking at paintings, and return in time for the tutorial. It was putting off the essay, but there was time enough for that the following day, when she had no classes.

She thought of what had been said in the lecture. The Auden poem was absolutely right: the message about suffering was there, underneath the depiction of the pastoral scene, but she felt that she would have been unaware of it had it not been pointed out to her. That had happened to her so often – before she had learned how to read the references that painters used. She had been given a dictionary of subject and symbol in art, and that had changed everything.

She made her way towards George IV Bridge. Her thoughts turned now to the flat, and about how well the sharing arrangements were working. She and Georgia were closer now, and Angela seemed to have got over her initial reservations about Georgia. Both of the other young women seemed to get on well enough with Neil and Ian, and with James too, although they saw very little of him. She herself liked Ian, but felt that she was never likely to get particularly close to him. It was different with Neil. He was more outgoing and she found him rather intriguing. At times his manner was almost flirtatious, but she felt that this was misleading. There were some people who gave the impression they were interested when they were not. Sometimes it was just the way they talked, as was the case with some Glaswegians, who could sound as if they were about to start a fight or proposition you – one could take one's pick of intentions. She grinned at the impermissible thought; she knew she should not even *think* such a thing.

She passed the entrance to Greyfriars Kirk. Scotland's religious history was everywhere, she thought; Greyfriars kirkyard housed a monument to the Covenanters, who stood out against an attempt to compromise their strict reformation, and were prepared to die in the process. Scotland's history was so bloody, with scheming and warring nobles and wild, unruly Highland clans. That had all been swept away by the passage of centuries, but she felt that some of the violence had not been entirely eradicated. It was still there, she thought, like a recalcitrant stain on an item of clothing; still there in the newspaper pictures of the picket lines of miners and police staring at one another – tinder that was only too ready to be ignited. She thought of suffering, and its curious banality; it persisted, surviving all our attempts to consign it to the past; closer to us than we imagined, the backdrop to our innocent activities, our lack of attention. Nobody would notice Icarus falling, even today; he would simply be another microlight casualty, nothing more than that. She thought for a moment of how the myth might be told today: Daedalus gives his son, Icarus, a hang-glider. He warns him that he should avoid flying too high, where strong winds might collapse the structure. Icarus is a daredevil, though, and ignores the advice. The hang-glider suffers structural failure and he falls into the sea. She smiled to herself. That was the beauty of Greek myths – their message being universal, they could very easily be adapted to any age and any setting.

She stopped. A short distance ahead of her, she saw James crossing the road. He was with someone – a young woman – and when he reached the pavement, he and his companion made their way into a large coffee bar, popular with students. For a few seconds, she wondered whether she had been mistaken, but she decided that it had definitely been James. The young woman with him was the girl Mrs Donald had sent to ask about the room, she thought. It was definitely her; it was the apprentice chef, Lizzie, from the North British Hotel – the woman who was seemingly so good at making mayonnaise. Julie was surprised; James had not been in the flat when Lizzie had come round to ask about the room, and she could not think of how the two of them might have met. Then she remembered that James had said something about taking mail round to Mrs Donald, and Lizzie, she knew, was employed there as an occasional cleaner.

Julie was suddenly curious. Were they on a date? They seemed an unlikely couple: the urbane New Yorker, with his expensive education, and this rather ordinary young Scotswoman with her apprenticeship and her mayonnaise. They came from two quite different worlds.

And yet, why else would they be going into the coffee bar together? She struggled: it was none of her business – she understood that – but at the same time it was perfectly natural to be curious about the people with whom one shared a flat. And there was no harm in satisfying her curiosity in a discreet fashion. They would not see her if she slipped into the coffee bar after them, and, even if they saw her, there would be nothing to explain: if what they were doing was none of Julie's business, then what she for her part was doing was no concern of theirs.

The coffee bar, stretching the full depth of the solid tenement building, consisted of several large rooms, one of which, being L-shaped, made for a quite separate area at the back. It was busy, and as usual full of students, who were capable of spinning a single cup of coffee out over a period of two hours or more, while they read or wrote their essays at the café's pine tables. It was noisy – full of the sound of a score of different conversations, each vying with one another to be heard.

While she ordered her coffee, Julie glanced over her shoulder to where the two of them were sitting, at the far end of the room. They had found a free table and had claimed it, their chairs drawn in close together.

She found a place at a table that was already occupied, but at which there were two spare seats. The current occupants made it clear that they did not mind her joining them. "This place gets too busy sometimes," said one of them, a thin young man with scholarly round spectacles.

"And too noisy," said his companion, a small, rather mousey young woman with a pedantic, slightly disapproving style of speaking.

Julie made a non-committal response. It was not that she did not want to join a conversation; her focus was on what was happening at a table on the other side of the room. James was sitting forward in his seat, talking to Lizzie with the intensity of one who has something important to say. Even had they not been holding hands across the table, it would have been impossible to form any impression other than that these two were lovers.

Julie brought her gaze back to her own table – to the cup of coffee steaming before her. She lifted it to her lips before stealing another quick glance at James and Lizzie. Why should she be surprised? Lizzie was an attractive young woman, whose occupation as an apprentice chef was rather different from what one expected of people in this part of town, who were mainly students. And for his part, James had the glamour of the exotic – a New Yorker, far from home, a philosopher, good-looking in a fairly conventional way.

She reflected that in the last few weeks she had seen very little of James. He seemed to keep different hours from everybody else in the flat, and when he was in he tended to sequester himself in his flat. He had a dissertation to write, of course – he had tried to explain to her what it was about but she had found it difficult to disentangle the technical terminology. He had sensed this, and had said, with a slightly mischievous smile, "It's about philosophy, actually." And she had returned the smile, and said, "I see." Now she wondered why James had not said anything about seeing Lizzie. It occurred to her that he might be ashamed of her; they were a group of people who had at least one thing in common: they were all students. He might think that Lizzie was somehow beneath them intellectually; he might even imagine that their view would be that he was somehow taking advantage of this less worldly girl; that his interest would be in conquest, rather than in an equal relationship. She did not think it likely that he thought this, as he seemed a very straightforward, unpretentious person, who would not be concerned about his image or the way that others might think of him.

She drank her coffee quickly, even if it had been served too hot.

"You look as if you're in a hurry," said the young man with the round glasses.

She dabbed at her lips with a handkerchief. It bore the stains of the previous cup of coffee. "Not really." She looked at her watch. She was not sure that she would have time now to go the National Gallery. That did not matter – the paintings would be there next week.

She made an effort to say something to her table companions. She did not want to be thought rude. "Are you at uni?" she asked.

The other two nodded. "History," said the young man.

"And I'm doing psychology," said his friend.

The young man smiled. "She knows how people feel," he said. "She understands how people's minds work."

Julie laughed. "I suppose that's what psychology's about."

She gave the young woman an appraising look. She noticed that she was wearing a light red jacket that looked as if it might have been part of a trouser suit. It had a dated appearance. It was from the sixties, she decided. And then, as the young woman shifted in her seat, Julie smelled the fabric. There was the unmistakeable smell of mothballs. "Armstrong's," she muttered.

The young woman looked puzzled. "What?"

Julie had intended her remark as an aside – made to herself, rather than to anybody else.

"Did you buy your jacket at Armstrong's?"

The young woman's face broke into a broad grin. "Of course. Who doesn't get their stuff there?"

"I don't," said the young man. "The men's clothes are gross. Thick, heavy tweed. Trousers with turn-ups. Everything belonged to people who are dead now." He wrinkled his nose. "That's how they get a lot of their things, you know. They do clearances of people's houses after they've died. That's why it's all so retro. The people who owned those things are so retro that they're dead."

The young woman laughed. "That's seriously retro."

Julie said, "Mothballs. Some of the clothes they sell have been stored with mothballs. You smell it as you go in."

The young woman frowned. She sniffed at her sleeve. "Not this, I think."

Julie said nothing.

"You were looking at those people," the young woman said, nodding in the direction of the table at which James and Lizzie were sitting. "I wondered why. I know it's none of my business, but I wondered why."

Julie was taken aback. She had been unaware that her interest had been so obvious. She hesitated before she answered. "He's my flatmate. One of them."

The young woman looked across the café. "And he's with that girl . . . Is that the problem?"

"It's not a problem," Julie said quickly. "I was just surprised."

"And you like him, I take it. You fancy him, even."

Julie gave her a discouraging look. "I don't, actually."

"Because you can tell when somebody is jealous. It's one of the easiest emotions to read."

Julie drew in her breath. "I'm not jealous."

"But you still wish she wasn't there – am I right?"

Julie shook her head. "I've got nothing against her. I've only met her once."

"Well, maybe I'm wrong," said the young woman. "I'm not always right."

"Almost always," interjected the young man. "You're almost always right, Jenny."

Julie looked at her watch again – pointedly now. "I have a tutorial at twelve," she said.

"On what?" asked the young man.

"I study history of art," explained Julie.

"Do you enjoy it?" asked the young woman.

"Yes. I love it."

There was a silence. Julie rose to go.

"Good luck," said the young woman.

"Good luck with what?" Julie asked herself. But to the young woman – Jenny – she said, "Thank you."

She moved away from the table, feeling the eyes of her two new acquaintances follow her. She felt empty. James might have told her that he was going out with Lizzie. Did he really think that she – or anybody else for that matter – would judge him? None of them was a snob, although Georgia might, just might, be on the borderline when it came to these things. She felt a slight sense of betrayal. It would have been no effort for him just to walk down the corridor and tell her that he was now seeing the Mayonnaise Assistant. It would not have been a complicated thing to speak about. People said that sort of thing to their friends every day. Hers certainly did, in what they called their *goss* sessions. *I like so-and-so. He's asked me out. I fancy him.* Nothing was at stake here – it would just have been nice to know. That was all.

Fifteen

Just sleep, okay?

IAN HAD WALKED PAST the bar in College Street many times before – it was cheek by jowl with one of the main university buildings – but had not taken particular notice of it. It had a narrow frontage, and its signs, one painted on the stonework across the frontage and the other a small board suspended above the entrance, were discreet and weathered. The Captain's Bar consisted of a single room stretching back the whole depth of the building. On one side was a long mahogany bar behind which were brewers' mirrors, a range of bottles, and the ornate taps of the draught beers. There were benches along the other wall, and leather-covered stools at the bar itself, but for the most part the clientele stood in small clusters, students and locals alike. The ceiling, high, as almost all Edinburgh ceilings were, was stained yellow with the deposited tars of years of smoke. There was a certain rough vigour about it; the customers now included women, but the bar seemed to make no concessions to femininity. In that respect, The Captain's Bar was part of a tradition of Scottish bars that was very different from the welcoming warmth of an English pub. This was where, in the past, men came to talk to other men, and to drink whisky.

Ian had never particularly liked bars. He would from time to time meet his fellow students in pubs, but he had never taken to standing at a bar. If he wanted to meet friends, he far preferred a coffee house of the sort that were now beginning to proliferate in the city. But Stewart, his closest friend at school, was going to be in Edinburgh and had asked if they could meet in The Captain's.

"You know the place?" Stewart had said.

"I know where it is," replied Ian.

"It's a great bar," said Stewart. "I was there last time I was in Edinburgh. Easy to get to. You can hear yourself speak – unlike some places. Let's meet there."

Stewart was studying economics at St Andrews. He was not enjoying the course, and was thinking of changing, but was yet to decide what to choose as an alternative. Ian had not seen him since they had parted company at the end of their last year at school. There had been plans to meet on one or two occasions, but they had never materialised. Then Stewart had called Ian unexpectedly, to tell him he was coming down to Edinburgh for an interview for a work placement, and would have time on his hands. He suggested The Captain's, and the arrangement was made.

Ian arrived first. He ordered a drink and stood at the end of the bar. Stewart had always been punctual, and Ian expected that he would not have to wait much more than ten minutes. He looked about him, feeling awkward that he was by himself and everybody else, as far as he could see, was in a group. He stared down into his glass and tried to remember how they had parted on that final day at boarding school.

"I'll see you some time in the summer," Stewart had said. "Perhaps we could go somewhere. I'd like that."

Ian's heart skipped a beat. "Yes. So would I." He paused.

"What about Italy? You can get these rail passes. You can travel as far as you like."

"Great," said Stewart. He frowned. He had thought of something. "I'm not sure, though. My folks are talking about going to Canada. My dad's brother is there – in Toronto. They've been talking for ages about going to see him. My uncle has a cottage on a lake. I've seen photographs. They have a couple of canoes that the Canadians use – you know the type. They're quite wide."

"So you'll go too?" asked Ian.

"Yes. Me and my sister." His sister was in her second year at the University of Aberdeen. She was a pianist.

"Of course." Ian knew Janet from the occasions when he had gone with Stewart and his family on summer trips. He would have liked all that to continue, but he knew it would not. It was too late now for friends to be taken on those family holidays.

Nothing more was said about Italy, and he realised it would not happen. They had stood there in the quad, along with others, waiting to go into the chapel for the final service of the term. It would be attended by parents, and there would be a lunch afterwards, with speeches. And then the pipe band lined up outside and they started to play: some of the girls cried; some of the boys fought back tears too. The pipers had at least their work to do; the music could express how they felt.

They went their separate ways, and he suddenly found himself getting into his father's car and realising that he had not said a proper goodbye to Stewart. But it was too late, as he could see that he had already left.

"A bit sad?" asked his father from the driver's seat.

He fixed his gaze on the hills behind the playing fields, and on the sky above them, which was largely cloudless now, as it was one of those rare days in Scotland when the air was still and there was no sign of rain. A few wisps of white hung in the upper atmosphere – ice crystals falling in attenuated curtains.

His father asked, "Are you all right?"

He replied that he was, although he felt as if he was choking. It was an effort not to cry, and he struggled to suppress the sobs that he knew were just below the surface. Because this was the end of a chapter that he did not want to end, because he feared that he would never again make such friends as he had made at school, and one friend in particular. It would have been different had he been able to talk about it, but he could not do that because there was nobody who would understand. You should not feel all that sad about saying goodbye to friends – you should not. You should not make such a big thing of ordinary friendships, because if you did that you were bound to be hurt when they came to an end, as friendships did.

He had come across some lines of Burns that seemed to him to resonate with the loss he felt. It had been a moment of recognition. Here was Burns saying the things that he, all these years later, felt in the depths of his soul. *We twa had paidled in the burn, from morning sun til dine, but seas between us braid hae roared* . . . Broad seas had come between us since then – that would happen; he was sure of it. At least Burns understood. At least he knew how friendship could be a bittersweet thing – something precious and yet at the same time something that seemed destined to end. Which was what our human lot amounted to. We were alive, but we knew we were dying. Everything we made about us was ultimately impermanent. We were the inhabitants of a dying planet.

"You have a lot to look forward to," said his father.

He nodded. That was undoubtedly true. But he felt his loneliness like a weight upon him, unshifting, always there. Other people had the freedom to be themselves, safe in the knowledge that there was no reason for others to disapprove of them. It was different for him. He was somebody who felt at odds with the world as it was, even as he had to pretend that he accepted the whole edifice of expectations and beliefs by which most people lived. His father was an understanding man – not somebody who was harsh or censorious. And yet his father did not know what his own son wanted in life. He did not know. He stared out of the window. People did not know, but that was because he did not tell them. And yet it was not easy to tell others when for some reason or other the time never seemed quite right. Or when you felt that what you had to tell them was exactly what they did not want to know. Or when – and this was possible, it occurred to him – they already knew what you had to tell them, but could not, for their own part, tell you that they knew.

He turned. He had felt Stewart's presence even before his friend said anything, in the way in which we know some things. There he was, standing behind him, holding a small overnight bag that he put down on the floor before he offered to shake hands.

And it was just a handshake. He wanted it to be an embrace. He wanted to wrap his arms around his friend and hug him, rather than restrict himself to this restrained, polite gesture.

He wanted that, but he did not do it. He moved forward slightly, though, which would have to do. There could be no embrace between friends in The Captain's Bar.

Stewart said, "You found it."

He replied, "Yes. I've walked past this place often enough."

Stewart looked about him. "I like these old places."

Ian wondered whether this was how it would be. He wondered whether their conversation would be limited to these banalities – to small talk – when he wanted so much to talk about other things. Had Stewart changed? Would he no longer be interested in the sort of things they talked about when, at school, it seemed so important to discuss those big issues of how one might lead one's life.

He ordered Stewart a beer. When it came, they raised their glasses to one another.

"It's been a long time," said Stewart.

He nodded. "Yes. Ages. Sorry."

Stewart shook his head. "No, I'm the one who should say sorry. I meant to be in touch, but you know how it is."

Ian smiled. "Life gets in the way."

"Jeez," said Stewart, "doesn't it just?" He paused, and looked about the bar. "Odd place this, isn't it? Those old guys look as if they're built in with the furniture."

"Yes."

"Then, those boys over there . . ." Stewart nodded to a group of four young men standing near the door. "They're law students. The law faculty's just across the road, isn't it? I recognise one of them. His brother was at Coll with us. Remember him? A guy called Pritchard."

Coll was how they referred to the school.

"Pritchard? He was a swimmer, wasn't he?"

Stewart nodded. "Won everything. Played the guitar – badly."

Ian laughed. "Everybody played the guitar badly. It was sort of expected, wasn't it?"

Stewart did not answer. Ian noticed that he glanced at his watch. Then Stewart said, "I never think about those days, you know. Or hardly ever. Now and then, I suppose, when I meet one of the guys, but . . ." He shrugged. "Some people keep up with the people they knew there, but I'm not really one of them." He stopped. "Of course, you're different. I mean, we go back a long way, don't we? How many times did you come on holiday with us? Four?"

"Something like that. Yes, four, I suppose."

"That was great," said Stewart. Then he frowned. "My mother had the idea that you were unhappy. I suppose it's because you lost your mum. I suppose that was why she thought that. But I never thought you were, you know."

Ian said nothing.

"I told her you were fine," Stewart continued. "I told her that you had got over it and were . . . well, you were just like everybody else – getting on with things."

Ian lifted his beer glass to his lips. Across the room, the law students laughed at something.

"Colonsay," Stewart continued. "Do you remember it?"

Ian lowered his glass. "Of course. That house your folks rented."

"Yes. I love that island, you know. I'd like to go back some time. In fact, I think I might even try to get over there later this summer. Just for a few days. Get the ferry over from Oban and go for a walk to that bay – the one where we caught a whole stack of mackerel."

Ian hesitated. "I'd like that."

"You too?"

"Yes." Ian paused. "Going back to places you were happy in – well, I think it works. Not always, but often, perhaps."

Stewart took a sip of his beer. "You're right. I'm going to speak to Kirsty. Talking about it has made my mind up. Colonsay it is. Maybe camping. I'll speak to her about it."

Ian looked down at the floor.

"She's at St Andrews too," Stewart said. "We've been going out for six months. She's great."

Ian nodded. "That's good."

"You should come up to St Andrews some time and meet her. You'd like her. Just let me know."

"I will."

Stewart brushed a strand of hair from his brow. "I need to get to the barber. There's this Turkish guy I go to. Except he's a Kurd, he tells me. He gives you a close shave if you want, although these days they don't use the cut-throat razor. Just as well." He shuddered.

"Oh, well," Ian muttered, unsure as to what was expected of him here.

"I've bought a car," Stewart said. "Or rather, my dad bought it for me. It wasn't expensive because it's twenty-five years old. It's a Morgan. Have you ever been in one?"

Ian shook his head.

"Their suspension is fantastic," said Stewart. "It gives you a really firm ride. A Morgan always hugs the road."

"Do they?"

"The bodywork is made of ash, you know," Stewart continued. "They're wooden cars – well, partly wooden."

"Amazing."

"Yes. The gearbox is a bit rough, but you always get that with an old car. God, it drives really well. I drove over to Ullapool the other day. The road was almost empty. It was fantastic weather. The sky was empty – not a single cloud . . ."

And Ian thought, we walked along that road on Colonsay. We walked for miles – right to the other side of the island. It was a day like that, and there was no wind, which meant the sea was calm – like a blue field stretching out to the distant horizon, to other islands we could not see . . . There was a fishing boat, and a line of wake behind it, and gulls circling above it for the scraps. The gorse was in flower – patches of yellow against the green – and it smelled of coconut. You said that. I remember it. You said: There's a smell of coconut from those flowers – just like coconut, but they're gorse, aren't they?

Ian walked back across the Meadows. It was a warm night, and there were small groups of people still sitting out on the grass, although the light had largely gone from the sky. From one group, huddled under a tree, came the sound of laughter and the tuneless strumming of a guitar. Another bad player, he thought; the country was full of bad guitarists. He strained his eyes against the darkness, trying to make out the figures. He saw the shape of the guitar. He saw that a couple of the people listening were sprawled out on the grass. Two figures lay together, arms about one another. A small point of light showed where somebody was smoking. He would have liked to go across and ask them if he could join them, if he too could sit down on the grass and talk about whatever it was that they were talking about, and feel happy in their friendship.

He thought of the half-hour he had spent with Stewart in The Captain's Bar. It had been a very bad idea, and he should have come up with some excuse. Stewart would not have minded had he called off, because the meeting had not seemed at all important to him. You can tell by the look in people's eyes if they would like to be somewhere else. It always shows. They're just not there – or not altogether there.

It was obvious that Stewart did not regard the friendship they had had as being anything significant. Why should he? When you were young, friends were easily made and just as easily abandoned. And even if the friendships at that stage in life were intense ones, it was a mistake to regard them as profound. They were, by their very nature, transitory – preparations for something else, something more important that would come later – if you were fortunate. Those intense friendships were like little love affairs, although they were completely innocent. You could easily think of nothing but your friend. You could easily want to spend every waking moment in his company. And then suddenly it might be as if a door had closed and the friend was no longer your be-all and end-all.

For a brief moment he had imagined that Stewart was inviting him to go with him to Colonsay. For a brief moment he had entertained the thought that it might be possible once again to spend time with his friend in that place that was inextricably linked with happiness, and sun, and the smell of gorse. But he had been quickly disabused of that notion, and he was back in a present in which Stewart had grown away from him; in which he seemed like a stranger; and in which he belonged to somebody else.

Ian felt almost light-headed. He felt that he had brought

something to an end. He had closed a chapter, which was the right thing to do, and he felt relief at having taken a decision. He did not mean anything in particular to Stewart – he was just somebody he had known when he was younger – that was all. This was no David and Jonathan friendship – and perhaps it never had been, other than on his side, perhaps. It was unequal, as so many friendships are. He had thought that he had something, but it was illusory. Stewart had no inkling of what their friendship had meant – he was incapable of understanding it.

By the time he reached the flat, his mood had changed. Now he felt an emptiness within himself – the sort of surprised emptiness that comes when one is subjected to rejection or rudeness. He had not felt that when he had left the Captain's, nor when he was crossing the Meadows, but it came upon him now as he climbed the stairs to their landing at the top. And when he entered the flat and made his way to his room, it was even worse. He was not sure who was in, but the kitchen and the living room were both in darkness. People could be out – it was still relatively early – or they could be in their rooms. There was no sound of anybody.

He went into the kitchen and switched on a light. The table had a couple of dirty plates on it – somebody had forgotten to wash these up, or had simply not bothered to do so. Georgia was the main culprit in that regard – Julie had made one or two pointed remarks about people who left things lying about, but they had had no effect. "She probably had somebody at home to clear things up," Julie muttered. "I'm not pointing the finger, but it looks like that." Now Ian made himself a cheese sandwich. He had a loaf of bread in his cupboard – they each had personal storage space – and he had a block of strong Cheddar in the dairy compartment of the fridge. He cut a couple of slices of bread before opening the fridge to find his cheese.

His eye was caught by a small jar on the middle shelf of the fridge. He had not seen it before. It was painted in bright colours, in the style of a Clarice Cliff ceramic, and it had a spoon sticking through a slot in the lid.

He peered at the jar and then took it out to investigate. Opening the lid, he saw the thick creamy substance in which the spoon had been inserted. He dipped a finger into the jar. He did not think before he did this – it was as if it were an automatic response. And then he raised the finger to his lips and tasted the small yellow-white dab he had extracted. He wrinkled his nose as he tasted the sample. Then, on impulse, he reached for the spoon, dipped it further into the jar, and extracted a spoonful. This he spread on one of the pieces of bread that he had cut. There would be cheese to be added to that, and he would then have his sandwich. He did not think of the unwritten rule that everybody in the flat understood – that you did not eat other people's food without their permission. Mayonnaise was different. He would not have eaten somebody's pie or anything like that – but this was simply taking a smidgeon, a taste, that could not possibly be missed by whoever owned the mayonnaise? Georgia? Possibly. She liked sauces and had jars of things like tahini or Greek taramasalata that she kept in the fridge.

He sat at the kitchen table and ate his sandwich. It did not take long, and within a couple of minutes he was at his door. As he switched on the light inside, Neil came by in the corridor.

"You've been out?" Neil asked.

Ian nodded. "I was in The Captain's Bar."

Neil knew the place. He now said, "Meeting friends?"

Ian hesitated. "A friend. Somebody I knew at school."

Neil watched him. He waited for Ian to say something more, but he did not. Nor did he step further into his room.

"Are you all right?" Neil asked. "You look . . . Well, you look a bit down."

Ian met Neil's gaze. "Do I?" His voice was unsteady.

Neil moved forward. "To be honest, yes. Has something happened?"

"I'm all right." Ian turned away. "It's nothing."

Neil's voice showed his concern. "Can I come in?"

Ian did not resist. "I'm all right," he repeated. But now he moved aside to allow Neil to come into his room. He closed the door behind them. He indicated for Neil to sit on the chair at his desk while he sat down on the bed.

Neil fixed him with an enquiring gaze. "Do you want to talk?"

"About?"

Neil shrugged. "About anything you like." He smiled. "The weather? The miners' strike?"

Ian smiled weakly. "The strike . . ." he began, but did not finish the sentence.

"Yes," said Neil. "It's getting brutal, isn't it?" He paused. "But I suspect that's not what's bugging you. It's something else."

"It's everything," said Ian. "Everything."

Neil looked doubtful. "Existential angst? The state of the world? I don't think so. Everybody lives with that. You get by in spite of all that, don't you think?"

When Ian did not reply, Neil continued, "We've lived with the threat of being blown to bits all our lives. The Cuban

Crisis and so on – not that we were around at the time, but our folks were. My parents said there were a few days when they were convinced that it was the end. People were given a leaflet telling them to take shelter under the kitchen table. We've lived with that, but we carry on with our lives, don't we? It's like living under a volcano. You act as if it isn't there – because if you don't, you can't lead any sort of life."

"No," said Ian. "I suppose not."

"So it's not that, then," Neil continued. "It's personal, isn't it?" He paused again. "Look, it's none of my business. I don't want to pry. We all have issues. We all have things that get us down. And we often don't want to speak about them – which is fine. But we shouldn't let them make us too miserable."

Ian sat back, then lay out on his bed. He put his hands behind his head and stared up at the ceiling. "Do you ever get the feeling that you're waiting for life to start?"

Neil frowned. "I'm not sure. It depends what you mean. I sometimes feel that I'm not sure where life is taking me, so to speak. I sometimes wonder whether I'm on the right track – or any track at all."

"I know what you mean," said Ian. "And I just feel . . . well, I feel that I'm a bit lost, I suppose I know that sounds pathetic, but it's true. I just feel a bit unhappy. And it gets me down from time to time. Maybe it shouldn't, but it does."

"Like now?"

Ian nodded. He closed his eyes. "Yes," he said. "Really badly. I feel really on my own."

There was a silence. Then Neil said, "You aren't you know. You've got all of us. Me, Julie, Angela. All of us. We live with you. You aren't on your own."

"I know, but . . ." muttered Ian.

Neil got up off his seat. Crossing the room, he switched off the light. "It's easier to talk in the dark," he said.

Ian said nothing.

Then Neil was beside him. "Move over," he said. "Give me a bit of room."

They lay side by side in the darkness.

"Just this," said Neil. "Just this, okay?"

Ian remained silent.

"Just company," said Neil. "Do you mind?"

"No, of course not."

"And we can talk," said Neil. "About anything – it doesn't matter. And if I stop answering, you'll know I've gone to sleep." Neil kicked off his shoes. "Take your shoes off," he said. "Go on. I don't want you to kick my shins at two in the morning."

There was light from the night sky. There were shadows on the ceiling. Outside, somewhere in the distance, a siren wailed and then faded.

They talked, but not for long. Neil's voice revealed his drowsiness. After not much more than ten minutes, it faded altogether. Ian heard his breathing. He looked at his friend's face in the darkness; we are all so vulnerable in repose, the proudest of us, the most blessed, the most unfortunate are much the same – there is complete equality in sleep. He shifted slightly to give him more room. He felt a strange joy at Neil's presence. The world was kinder now, it seemed to him, although he knew that this would not be repeated. This was an unplanned, spontaneous act of friendship on Neil's part, but it was for this moment, and this moment only.

He watched the shadows on the ceiling. He felt sleep come over him. In the small hours, he awoke briefly. Neil had shifted in his sleep. His arm was over Ian's shoulder, innocently, protectively. Ian did not move it.

And his friend's arm was there when they woke up in the morning to see Julie at the door. It had not been closed properly, and a slight breeze from an ill-fitting Victorian window somewhere else in the flat nudged it open during the night. She had been walking down the corridor and had stopped at the open door. She stood quite still as she took in the room, the bed, the two of them, still fully clothed but in each other's arms. She said, "Oh, I'm sorry," and moved away.

Ian looked at Neil. "The door," he said.

Neil scratched the back of his head. "I was deeply asleep. I must have been tired."

"Julie?" said Ian.

Neil shrugged. "So what?" he said.

Sixteen

Are you serious? No.

THAT MORNING, WHEN NEIL went into the kitchen to make his breakfast, Angela and Georgia were both already there. Angela was finishing a bowl of muesli, scraping the last oat flakes from the bowl; Georgia was spreading marmalade on a slice of underdone toast. Angela had switched on the radio and was listening to the news. Georgia had an open magazine lying on the table in front of her.

They both looked up when Neil came in.

"You're looking dishevelled," said Georgia.

Angela gave him a cursory look. "He hasn't shaved."

Neil shrugged. "Why should I? Shaving's a form of repression targeted at men. We're enslaved to the razor. Look clean-shaven if you want a job. Whatever you do, don't look as nature intended you to look."

Angela laughed. "Nice try, Neil. You didn't shave because you couldn't be bothered. Admit it. You're lazy."

"Or giving up," Georgia suggested.

Neil smiled. "What if I said to you that expecting men to shave was like expecting women to wear make-up?"

Angela's response came quickly. "I'd say false equivalence."

Georgia chuckled. "I'd say the same thing – once I'd looked the words up."

Neil cut himself a slice of bread. "I'm going to shave. It's just that . . ." He did not finish. Julie came into the room. She stopped, only for the briefest moment, but Neil noticed. She had not expected to see him – and he had not thought he would see her. Julie often had nine o'clock lectures and was first out of the flat in the mornings.

Angela looked up. She pushed her empty bowl to one side. Georgia, closing the magazine she had been paging through, said, "This is rubbish. Pure gossip. These people do nothing but have their photographs taken. They're airheads."

"Of course they are," said Angela. "That magazine is for people who've got nothing better to do than follow what happens to these useless celebs." She paused. "Who bought it?"

Julie seemed relieved to be involved in the conversation. She had glanced at Neil, and then looked quickly away. The magazine was a welcome distraction. "I've never bought that trash," she said.

"Don't look at me," said Georgia. "I found it here. It was over there, near the bread bin."

"It wasn't me," said Angela. "I wouldn't be caught dead reading that."

Julie crossed the room to a cupboard. She took out a mug. She was famous for her frugal breakfast – a cup of black coffee and a single oatcake spread with marmalade. Over her shoulder she said, "So, if it wasn't me, nor Angela, nor Georgia, that means it's one of the boys." She addressed Neil over her shoulder, still not making eye contact with him. It was obvious to Neil that had either of the other two been paying attention to what was going on, they would have detected the electric current of awkwardness crackling between him and Julie.

"Not me," he said. "I admit I've seen that mag before, but not here. And I doubt if James—"

Georgia interrupted him. "Oh, James is far too serious for that sort of thing. He left *The Philosophical Quarterly* in here the other day. Next to the butter. I had a read of it – well, a couple of pages. There was an article about shared responsibility. I became quite involved."

Angela looked interested. "You mean, whether we're responsible for things that are done in our name?"

"Collective responsibility," said Neil. "There are some tricky questions there. Who was responsible for what happened under the Nazis?"

"That would depend," said Georgia. "People would have to look at what you did. There were plenty of people – Germans – who opposed Hitler, and nobody could blame them for what happened."

"Yet they still felt the consequences, didn't they?" said Angela. "And they couldn't really complain – because they were German, after all, and Germans had done those terrible things."

Neil threw a glance in Julie's direction. "What about the things *we've* done? Or our grandparents, for instance. Do we have to answer for colonialism and everything that went with it? Dispossession, land theft, the occasional massacre?"

"Nothing to do with me," said Angela. "I had nothing to do with that. And my parents and grandparents didn't either."

"But they benefitted from it," said Georgia.

Angela shook her head. "My grandfather was a miner. He went down the pits at fifteen. His own father, my great-grandfather was a miner too. He started even younger, I remember being told. They sent children down – children –

and made them carry coal in baskets."

Georgia winced. "I know . . ."

"And where did the money go?" Angela continued. "The profits from the coal? It went into the pockets of the owners – the people who owned the land. Those massive, big houses you see in the countryside – how were they built? Money from coal mines and from slave plantations in the West Indies. That's what paid for them."

"Nobody disagrees with you, Angela. But that's what happened everywhere in those days." She half-turned to Neil. "What do you think, Neil?"

He thought for a moment. "I'd probably agree with Angela. All that I'd say, though, is that it's not easy to disentangle what's rotten and what's all right when it comes to money. In a society like this, everything is tainted, I suspect, because of the unfairness of the past."

"Perhaps we should pay a bit more back," said Julie.

"That's what overseas aid is meant to do," said Georgia. "At least it's a start."

Julie ladled a couple of spoons of coffee into a percolator. She returned to the magazine. "I don't think James would have bought it. So that leaves Ian."

There was a brief silence, broken when Neil said, "Ian's the last person who'd read that stuff."

"How can we be so sure?" Georgia challenged. "I feel I don't know him all that well. Do you?"

Neil felt Julie's eyes upon him.

"I think I know him reasonably well." He kept his voice even.

Angela agreed with Neil. "It's unlikely. It's not his style."

Julie shrugged. "So it just appeared? Blew in?"

"Somebody's friend might have brought it in," said Georgia. "Has anybody had a visitor?"

They looked at one another. "I had somebody from my course in the other day," volunteered Neil. "But not anybody who would read that."

"And my cousin was here earlier this week," said Georgia. "He doesn't read anything very much, and I doubt if he'd read that mag."

"So we still don't know," said Julie.

"No," said Neil. "Mystery."

Georgia rose from the table. She stretched. "You know," she began, "sometimes I get the feeling that this place is . . . I don't know – maybe haunted or something. I get the feeling that I'm not alone."

"Your imagination," said Neil.

She shook her head. "Maybe. Perhaps I'm sensitive to these things. It's just that I get this feeling and the back of my neck tingles. I remember getting it in France once, when we were staying in a gîte that my parents had rented. I was reading a Patricia Highsmith novel at the time – one of her rather creepy ones. And I remember scaring myself silly. I felt that there was somebody there. There wasn't, of course – it was my imagination. This is almost the same feeling, but not quite. I just feel it."

Angela got up from the table too. "I'd like to sit about," she said. "But I can't. I have an essay to get in by four this afternoon."

She and Georgia left the kitchen, and Neil and Julie were now alone. Neil cleared his throat. "This morning," he began. "I wanted to speak to you—"

She cut him short. "I'm really sorry," she said. "I didn't mean to barge in. The door was open, you see."

She watched him. He's beautiful, she thought. He's perfect. And obviously that was why Ian liked him.

"I know," he said. "And I'm not expecting you to apologise for anything."

"It was as if I was . . ." She hesitated. "I felt that I had intruded."

"I told you," he said. "You don't have anything to apologise for. And all I wanted to say to you is that you might have formed the wrong impression."

She waited. She was not finding this easy.

"You see what happened," Neil continued, "is that Ian came back to the flat last night feeling a bit low. I could see that was how he was. I realised that he wanted to talk, and so that's what we did. It was late. We ended up talking to one another on the bed. That's all. We just talked. I could have got up and left but I didn't really want to leave him. I felt sorry for him, you see. So I stayed. And then it was morning, and you walked past the door, and you imagined what I think you imagined."

She stared at him. She had no doubt that he was telling the truth.

"I suppose I did jump to conclusions," she said. "But now that you've explained—"

"Not that I think you'd particularly disapprove if it were otherwise," Neil went on. "It doesn't matter how people feel about other people, does it? It's nobody else's business."

"Of course."

"And yet it might still matter that people don't form the wrong impression, if you see what I mean. I know it isn't important, but I don't think I'd want you to think I'm gay. That's nothing to do with how I feel about other people being gay. It's just that, well, I happen not to be myself."

She nodded. "I didn't think you were."

He seemed to relax. "I didn't mind staying with Ian last night, you know. It was . . . well, it was companionable. And why shouldn't it be? Why should we be so uptight about sleeping with people – I mean, sleeping in the sense of sharing a bed and no more? Men, in particular, get really worked up over that. They don't like to hug their friends. They don't like to comfort other men by putting their arms about them. Why?"

"Fear of physical intimacy?"

"Yes. Taboo. So we end up being unable to touch our male friends. Oh, maybe a pat on the shoulder – that sort of thing – but no hugging. No putting arms around them."

"No." She paused. "It's easier for women, I think."

"Oh yes," he agreed. "Women can hold hands and nobody raises an eyebrow." He made a gesture of acceptance. "Well, we are where we are." He glanced at his watch. "I was going to take a shower. I need to get in for a class in an hour."

"So do I."

"You're going to shower?"

There was only one working shower in the flat. The one in what they called the girls' bathroom had blocked and they were waiting for the plumber.

"You can use ours," said Neil. "It's fine."

"No, you go ahead."

He stood up. "We could share."

She did not say anything. She looked away, then looked back at him. "Do we need to save water?" she asked, and smiled.

"I'm serious," he said. "We live together. We're friends. Friends share."

"I thought you were joking."

"I'm not. Just shower. That's all."

"So you sleep with a boy – and shower with a girl."

Neil grinned. "Just sleep, just shower," he said, and then he added, "Actually, I wasn't being serious."

She felt confused, and disappointed. She turned away.

Seventeen

Relief distribution centre

IT WAS ALMOST AS if Angela had issued a challenge. "Come with me," she said. "Come and see what it's like." Georgia replied, "But I have been. I went with you and Ian."

"This is different," said Angela. "I'm going to do a stint at the relief centre. You might like to see what happens there."

Georgia did not argue. She felt that if she declined the invitation, Angela might conclude that she was in denial of what was happening. The strike was still on – the conflict, the bitterness, the suffering, it had all become more intense. There was no end in sight, and Georgia wondered whether the dispute would ever be resolved. She had decided that the miners would lose, sooner or later. And although she understood their side of the argument, she also understood what seemed to her to be a hard economic truth: there was no point in doing things for which there was no demand. If coal was no longer needed, then why produce more, simply because mining coal was what we had always done? She could not put it that way to Angela, but the thought was there. The world changed, and industries died. Yet now, in response to Angela's invitation, she decided she would go, rather than be accused of indifference or even hostility to a just cause.

Now they were walking along a road in Armadale, carrying two large bags they had picked up at the relief centre.

"These people," Angela said to Georgia, "are called Watson. He's Jim and she's . . ." She struggled to remember, then it came to her. "Ellen."

"Do you know them well?"

Angela shook her head. "We were at the same school. I haven't seen her for a while. I don't remember him at all – he would have been just one of the boys. We didn't mix a lot. But the girls all knew one another, and I remember her, although she was two or three years ahead of me. Three probably. And now . . ."

Georgia waited.

"Now here she is, living on this estate," Angela continued. "Two children already. She married at seventeen. Some girls married at sixteen. Sixteen! Can you imagine? The boys were usually a bit older."

On either side of them were small houses with postage-stamp gardens and short concrete paths that led to the front door. The gardens were, for the most part, neatly kept, although here and there was littered the detritus of children's play – a tricycle with a missing wheel, a toy plastic wheelbarrow piled high with sticks – and there were parked cars, too, some halfway up the paths, some on the road. A few revealed the pride of their owners, and had been kept clean, most bore the signs of wear.

Georgia remembered what she was like at seventeen. That she could have been married seemed inconceivable. The boys she knew at that age were so immature – *she* had been so immature herself and, given the different rate at which boys and girls grew up, they must have been even worse. To be committed at that stage to running a home, to becoming pregnant, to having one's freedom curtailed by the arrival of a child – well, that must be the end of your life before you even started it.

She shook her head. Angela, walking beside her, said that she could imagine what she was thinking. "It wouldn't have been for you, would it?"

Georgia winced. "Poor girls."

"Yes. And yet—"

"And yet what?" Georgia asked. "Could there be anything positive about it?"

Angela thought for a moment. "You'd go up the list for a house once there was a child. You'd have a place of your own. You'd be able to leave your parents, which you may be keen to do."

"I suppose so."

"And you'd be with somebody," Angela went on. "For a lot of people that's something really important. If you're living a middle-class life, of course, it's different. You have options. Other people don't. What's your future if you've left school with no qualifications? We're extremely fortunate – it's different for us."

Georgia was silent. She did not need to be reminded of the difference between her life and the life of the people Angela was talking about.

"We have everything," said Angela. "We have a sense of a future. We know what we want to do. We're getting an education. We don't have to get up each morning and think of how we're going to keep things going – how we're going to feed the children, how we're going to get to work, if we have a job, that is. All of that."

Georgia turned to her. "No, you're right. I get all that, you know."

Angela hesitated. Then she said, "I know you do."

Georgia might have continued, but she did not. We all have our prejudices, she thought; we all think that there are others who are stuck in their view of the world and who cannot see what it is like for others. Angela had been like that, she felt, but had come round to accepting that she, Georgia, did not have the blinkers that so often went with a background like hers. She did not need to labour the point now – they both understood that.

Angela looked at the numbers on the houses. They were almost there.

"It's number eighteen," she said. "This next one."

Now they stood before the house. It was one of the neater ones. The front door had a bright brass knocker fixed to it, and the window frames looked as if they had been recently painted. There was an air of domestic pride.

The knocker was for show – a dolphin that might have been hinged in the past, but was now corroded into immobility. There was a bell, though, and Angela rang this once they had put the bags they were carrying down on the ground. Georgia looked up at the window on the first floor, directly above the door. It was slightly open, and it allowed them to hear the sound of a child crying within. The child's crying continued for a short while, and then stopped. This was followed by the sound of an adult voice.

The door opened.

"Ellen? You remember me – Angela?"

The young woman at the door had a toddler at her feet. The child was hanging on to her legs, embracing them as she looked up suspiciously at the strangers on the doorstep.

It took Ellen a few moments to make the connection. Then,

"Oh aye, I remember you." There was a smile. "You could come in," Ellen continued. "You and—"

"This is Georgia," said Angela. "She's my flatmate from Edinburgh."

"You're living there now?" Ellen asked.

"Yes. I was staying with my folks here in Armadale, but I had to do the trip into Edinburgh each day. It became a bit much."

Ellen nodded, and moved aside to let them enter. They had picked up their bags, heavy with groceries. Ellen's eyes went to the bags.

Angela got straight to the point. "I was at the miners' relief office," she said. "I was talking to that woman down there, Mrs Edwards. You might know her."

"The tall one?" Ellen asked.

"Yes, that's her. She's on the committee. She told me that Jim had been ill and that you might have been finding things a bit difficult."

Ellen laughed. "Difficult? Oh, aye, it's difficult, right enough."

"I know," said Angela. "But there are folk on your side. And so we've brought some stuff. They gave us a list of things they thought you could find useful."

Ellen looked down at the bags. "It's not that I'm not grateful. I am. Things are really tight."

"I can imagine," said Georgia.

Ellen glanced at her. I am being judged by my accent, thought Georgia. It's the first ground of judgement – the very first typecasting that goes on and on and keeps everybody in their place. She felt herself blushing; it was so unjust, and it seemed that there was no escape from it. And now, she thought, this woman resents me. Here I am, bringing food, like Lady Bountiful dispensing largesse. Yet it was what was happening. It was part of the relief operation that had the union's blessing – and the approval of the community. It was not condescending charity – it was an ordinary, human response to need.

But if Ellen had been reserved, she now seemed to relax. "I could make you some tea," she said, adding with a wry smile, "At least we've got that."

"You wouldn't want to run out of tea," said Angela. "Thank you."

They were in the living room, the room into which the front door opened directly. In the cramped conditions of the small, terraced house, a hall would have been a waste of space.

They sat down – Angela on an easy chair and Georgia on a sofa over which a tartan rug had been spread. The rug was slightly stained. There was a carpet, worn smooth in places. There was an ash tray that needed emptying. A television set, silenced, stood against the wall. Some sort of gardening programme was on: a man using secateurs to cut a shrub. He soundlessly addressed the camera, showing a cutting that he had taken.

Ellen picked up the child before she left the room to make the tea. "She gets nervous when she's with people she doesn't know," she explained.

"What's her name?" asked Angela.

"Cheryl."

"Bonnie," said Angela. "She's very bonnie."

Georgia noticed the Scots word. This was Angela's world. She could say that a child was bonnie, but if she herself used the word it would seem all wrong. And she knew she should not try. You cannot be what you aren't. Words can be shibboleths – private to those who used them in their special way.

Ellen came back with tea served in two sturdy mugs, each bearing the legend *Scotland for the Cup.* They sipped at the tea, which was too strong for both of them. Ellen had, without asking, sugared it heavily. That, Georgia thought, must be the default position.

Angela started the conversation. "How are you doing, then?"

Ellen shrugged. "We're getting by," adding, "Just."

"It must be hard," said Angela.

"Aye, it's hard. But I'm not complaining. Some things have to be done."

"Of course they do," said Angela, looking at Georgia, as if providing her with a cue.

"The government has been planning this show-down," said Georgia.

Ellen looked at her with interest. "You think so?"

"Yes. They don't want coal."

Ellen made a dismissive sound – a *pah*. "They're happy enough to buy it from somewhere else."

"It's about our industrial base," said Angela. "They want to get rid of traditional industries. They want everybody to be more mobile – to go to where the jobs are."

Ellen shook her head vigorously. "There are no other jobs," she said. "And they don't care about us. Everyone knows that. I was at a talk the other day – down at the community centre. There was a man from France. He was some sort of official from their mining union. He said that the French government has at least tried to find other jobs for men from coalfields that are being closed down. That's the difference.

Their government cared. We're on the rubbish tip. There's nothing done for us."

"I know," said Angela. "The strikers have no alternative. They're out because they don't want to be down and out."

Ellen nodded. "I like that. Be out rather than down and out. Nice."

"It could be settled," said Georgia. "You never know."

Ellen looked doubtful. "I'm not so sure," she said. "I'd like to think you're right, but they seem to think they can starve us back to work. And then they'll close the pits. That man from the Coal Board, Ian MacGregor, has got a plan. Everybody says so."

Angela lowered her voice. "How's Jim doing?"

Ellen hesitated. "He's down. You know how it is when somebody sort of shrivels up inside. That's Jim. He's about the house a lot of the time. It's no place for a man during the day. He gets out. He does picket duty, but I worry for him. They're breaking heads, you know. I don't want my man coming home with a broken head."

"No," said Angela. "It must be scary for you."

"It is for everyone," said Ellen.

They sat in silence as they drank the cooling tea. To revive the conversation, Angela asked after people from school, but Ellen said that she was out of touch. The bairn, she said, took up most of her time, along with trying to run the house and make ends meet too.

"I should show you what we've brought," said Angela. "If there's anything you'd like to change, we can do that. We didn't want to bring you stuff that would be no use."

"I can use everything," said Ellen. "Don't worry about that."

They travelled back the way they had come – by bus. It was a slow journey, as the service was a local one, and passengers embarked or disembarked at numerous stops. It was evening now, and the sun was sinking in a red ball over towards the west, over Glasgow and its surrounds. West Lothian was a place of short distances and narrow roads.

"It's nice countryside," said Georgia. "It's lived in, isn't it?"

"You could say that," replied Angela.

"You must be very fond of it," said Georgia. "You must be fond of these villages and the people who live in them."

Angela nodded. "They're my people," she said.

Instinctively, Georgia reached out and took her hand. She pressed it. Angela returned the pressure, but then, although Georgia relaxed her hand, Angela did not let go.

"Thank you for coming with me," Angela said. "It's not your struggle, this."

Georgia was about to say she would never claim that it was. But Angela had more to say. "This is about whether we're going to continue to be a country that cares for people, or whether we're going to become a business. If we become a business, then there's no reason for the management to worry too much about us. It's all going to be about efficiency and profit."

Georgia looked out of the window. Angela was so certain; the rights and wrongs were all so clear to her. For her part, she wished she could be so certain; it would be easier. There was undeniable comfort in believing in something, and not doubting it. And yet she found it hard to ignore the rational part of herself – the part that saw the flaws in the trade union view of the world. *Don't try to be what you can never be*, she said to herself. *Don't try . . .*

She made as if to disengage her hand from Angela's, but her friend held tight. She tried again. At last, she said, "I don't think so."

Angela glanced at her and then looked fixedly out of the window. She released Georgia's hand.

"I don't mean to be unfriendly," said Georgia.

"No, it's fine. You don't have to say anything."

The bus continued its journey. Edinburgh came into view. Fields of ripening yellow oil-seed rape stretched away on one side of the road.

"So yellow," said Georgia. "Look at it. So yellow."

Eighteen

Not alone

THE FOLLOWING WEEK, DR Brock's Tuesday lecture was cancelled at short notice. The art historian, who was also a keen cyclist, had fallen off his bike while riding through Holyrood Park on the way in from his house in Portobello. His helmet had protected him from head injury, but his attempt to break his fall with his right arm had resulted in a painful fracture of a wrist bone and a trip to the accident and emergency department at the Royal Infirmary. Left with unexpectedly free time, Julie decided to spend the morning in the library, working on an essay that was due to be submitted the following week. On the way to the library, though, she discovered that she had left her library card in the flat, along with her purse. This was annoying, but since the flat was only a fifteen-minute walk across the Meadows, the situation was easily remedied. And it was a pleasant morning for a walk – sunny, yet not too hot – an attractive alternative to the still air and stuffiness of the library.

She made her way up the common stair, stopping briefly to exchange a few words with the woman who lived in one of the first-floor flats. She was in the process of locking her front door behind her, and briefly fumbled with a bunch of keys as she selected the right one. She was not sure of the woman's name, and their conversation had never progressed beyond a few banal observations. One day, she thought, she would say something that might nudge their exchanges into meaningfulness. She might ask her what she thought about the strike, for instance; or whether she believed in an afterlife; or whether the Buddhists were right in saying that responding to material appetites led only to unhappiness. You never knew – people might be yearning to break away from the superficiality that characterised our relationships with those we barely knew; but no, she decided she would never do that, although she might start by confessing to her that she had never learned her name. That might be a beginning of real human contact between them.

The flat would be empty, thought Julie. Tuesday was a day when everybody – at least, all the undergraduates – had morning lectures, and James had a three-hour seminar with his fellow postgraduates in the philosophy department. If she had the right books with her, she could easily have stayed in her own room and written her essay there – but there were library sources to be consulted. There were several articles in back issues of the *Burlington Magazine* that she needed to read, and a few other references that she would have to track down. She would pick up her library card and her purse and then be back in George Square by ten.

Once inside the flat, she closed the door behind her, but, as she did so, she dropped her keys on the floor. The keys made a sharp metallic sound as they landed, breaking the silence that had greeted her on her arrival. She bent down to retrieve them, and as she did so she heard a noise somewhere in the depths of the flat. She straightened up. Somewhere a chair was being pushed back, she thought – a rough, grating sound. Julie frowned: somebody was in the flat, one of her flatmates, she imagined, unless it was . . . There had been a break-in downstairs the previous week. Ground-floor flats were vulnerable, particularly from the drying green behind the building, and two youths had been seen climbing through a kitchen window. There had been a note from the police appealing for witnesses and warning people about security. She struggled to rein in her imagination. There was no sign that the front door had been tampered with, and surely there was no other way in which an intruder might have gained access to the flat. Perhaps the sound was nothing more than one of the entirely natural noises that a building makes: the rattling of a window sash in the wind; the expansion or contraction of a floorboard – buildings breathed, after all, and they were rarely completely silent.

She made her way towards the kitchen. Again, there came a sound – different, perhaps, from the last one, but now clearly enough a sign of human presence.

She approached the kitchen door. It was slightly ajar; now, edging towards it she was able to get a good view of the table, and there she saw James. He was sitting at the table, an open book in front of him, a mug of coffee at his side. Julie had been holding her breath; now she exhaled with relief.

"James?"

He looked up and smiled. "Well, good morning."

"I didn't think I'd find you in."

"No?"

She said that she thought he had his Tuesday seminar.

James hesitated. Then he shrugged. "Cancelled." There was another pause – as if he had thought better of what he had just said. "I mean, cancelled by me. I couldn't be bothered. The Tuesday seminar goes on far too long – even with the half-hour break we have in the middle. Some people like the sound of their own voice."

He leaned back in his chair, stretched out his arms, and yawned. It seemed to Julie that it was almost a theatrical gesture. "And you?" he said. "Don't you have anything?"

She explained how she had left her library card in her room and had come back to retrieve it. He glanced out of the window and observed that it was a nice morning for a walk.

There was a silence, broken when she said, "Is everything all right?"

For a moment he seemed taken aback by her question. Then he frowned and said, "Of course."

She nodded. "Sharing can be a bit odd sometimes, I think. We all have our separate lives, but we also have—"

"A common life?" he interjected.

"Yes, you could call it that." She paused. "It's a rather special time in one's life, isn't it? For most people, student years are the only time one will live in a community like this. You find yourself sharing with people you haven't met before and you . . . well, you become a member of something. And then, before you know it, it's over."

He nodded. "You're right," he said. "It's a short time of happiness."

She was struck by the expression. *A short time of happiness* . . .

He looked at his watch. "I'd better get back to work," he said. "The usual thing. My dissertation. I had hoped that it might write itself." He grinned. "They don't, do they?" He closed the book, and then rose from the table. "I'll see you later," he said. Then he added, "You must let me make you dinner some time. My specialty is cheese soufflé."

"I'd like that," said Julie. "Although soufflé's tricky, isn't it?"

"It's timing," said James. "You have to get your timing right. If not, a soufflé collapses."

He smiled at her and left the room. She stood where she was, looking down at the table, at the coffee mug that he had left there. He should have washed it, she thought. That was the rule: you washed the things you used; you did not leave them to be attended to by somebody else.

She picked up the mug and took it to the sink. As she did so, she noticed that there was another mug on the draining board. James, it seems, was not the only offender: Georgia often forgot to wash up; perhaps she had left it there after breakfast. She would have to wash that one too.

She picked it up. Immediately she noticed that the mug was half full. It was also warm to the touch. She dipped a finger into the coffee: it was not only warm – it was hot. This had been made recently – perhaps within the last ten minutes or so.

She stood quite still. There had been two people in the kitchen. One had left when she had unexpectedly arrived. James had not been alone. She looked down the corridor along which James had retreated to his room. She felt torn. Her natural curiosity made her want to confirm what she suspected, and yet another part of her urged her to mind her own business. If James chose to keep his personal life to himself, then that was his prerogative, and she should not pry. You did not eavesdrop on your flatmates; you respected their need for privacy.

Even as she thought this, she found herself inching her way down the corridor, as if drawn by some hidden force. She now felt a tinge of resentment. Why should James try to deceive her? For what he was doing amounted to deception, she thought. And it hurt her that he should want to keep somebody from her – Lizzie, she assumed.

She was now halfway down the corridor. She stopped. She thought she heard the sound of voices, but could not be certain. She strained her ears. Nothing. And then, once again, indistinctly but still audibly, somebody said something.

She turned away, suddenly mortified at her intrusion. She felt ashamed, and walked back down the corridor towards her own room. Within a few minutes, she had picked up her card and was letting herself out of the front door. A shaft of sunlight fell from the cupola above the stair. It shone off the walls, slanting, rich, like butter. She thought of James, of his smile and the warmth of his manner. If only it were different, but it was not. He was involved with somebody else and she should accept the fact that he wanted to exclude her from that part of his life. If you expected a closeness that was simply not there, then you were preparing nothing but a bed of sorrow and regret for yourself. She wanted to avoid that. She should not begrudge James whatever happiness this affair with Lizzie brought him. It was unlikely to last, after all, she thought: he would go back to New York and that would be that. She wondered whether Lizzie knew that. She was younger than the rest of them and she would not have had their experience. She would not necessarily have had the experience to know that at this stage of life, love affairs tended to be short-lived. But then she thought: I'm thinking that because I don't want it to last. I'm thinking that because I'm envious; and, once again, she felt ashamed.

She stopped. She had picked up something. She sniffed at the air. It was there, and there was no doubt about it. It was the smell of cologne – a faint but, to her, distinguishable smell, one that had attached itself to the fabric of the corridor as the person wearing it had walked past. She took a deep, slow breath, allowing the air to linger in the olfactory recesses. She tried to bring it to mind, and then it came: four, seven, eleven. Mrs Donald . . . Lizzie would have helped herself to her employer's cologne. Or been given it, of course. Either way, it confirmed what she suspected: Lizzie was there.

She found Angela in the coffee bar in the library basement. Angela was sitting with a couple of friends – a thin young man with a rather pinched, unhappy face, and a young woman in a blue shift dress and wearing Indian bangles up her arm. Julie caught Angela's eye as she found a seat for herself, and then waited. After a few minutes, Angela came over to join her.

"Something happened?"

Julie shook her head. "Nothing. Well, nothing serious. It's just that . . ."

Angela waited.

"It's just that I went back to the flat this morning. I'd left my library card in my room. I went back to get it."

"And?"

Julie told her about how she had heard what she thought was the sound of a chair being pushed back. She told her about the two coffee mugs. She did not mention the smell of cologne.

"There was something . . . something guarded about James's manner," she said. "I like him a lot, as you know. He's gentle. He's amusing. But he was jumpy this morning when I went in and he was not expecting me. I think he's hiding something."

Angela was cautious. "Oh, yes?"

"For some reason," Julie continued. "He doesn't want me to know that he's seeing Lizzie. Remember her? The mayonnaise person. I saw them together in a café. And now I'm pretty sure that she's spending a lot of time with him in the flat."

Angela smiled. "A whole lot of time," she said. "In fact, all the time."

Julie looked puzzled. "All the time?"

Angela did not reply immediately. She was staring at her hands. She seemed reluctant to explain.

"Are you saying . . ." Julie began.

Angela nodded. "Yes, I am. I think she's living there."

They sat in silence. Then Julie said, "Have you seen her?"

Angela lowered her voice. "I saw her coming out of the boys' bathroom. She didn't see me. The corridor light was off. She was wearing a T-shirt – and not much else. It was late at night. I was just about to go into the kitchen. I saw her going back into his room."

"Oh."

"And then," Angela continued, "I saw her down in the street once. She was by herself, and she was walking to the stair door down below. She didn't see me. She went in and I waited. Then I went to the bottom of the stair and looked up. I heard her unlocking our door at the top. She has a key – obviously."

Julie pursed her lips. It had not occurred to her that Lizzie was living with James, but now it seemed obvious. That would provide the reason for his secrecy. It was not because he was in any way ashamed of Lizzie – it was because he knew that their lease was inflexible on the point that only six people were to live in the flat. Julie had made that clear to everyone, and everyone had agreed. He was deliberately flouting a rule that they had all voluntarily accepted. She felt anger. This was cheating – it was as simple as that. It was a breach of trust. It was wrong.

It was a few minutes before she said anything. Then, "I think you're right. It all adds up, doesn't it?"

"Yes," agreed Angela. "It adds up."

Then Julie said, "How do you feel about it?"

Angela hesitated. It seemed to Julie that she was waiting for a lead from her.

At last, Julie said, "I feel a bit let down, to be honest."

"I'm not surprised."

"We all agreed. The lease spells it out. Six people – max."

"Yes," said Angela. "And now?"

Julie sighed. "I'm going to have to think about it." She paused. "What do you think we should do?"

Angela hesitated before replying. "I don't know if I want to do anything."

Julie frowned. Was Angela suggesting that it was her problem – and her problem alone?

Angela now went on. "I'm not trying to dodge anything," she said. "But we all look on you as being in charge. You signed the lease and so on."

Julie let out a long breath. This *was* a washing of hands. Angela was effectively saying that it had nothing to do with her. "All right," she said. "I understand. And I suppose you're right – it *is* my call. My name's on the lease. I'm the one who promised Mrs Donald that we would stick to six people."

"I don't want to sound as if I'm avoiding anything," said Angela. "I'll support you in whatever you decide to do."

Julie thanked her. It was half-hearted support, she felt, but it was at least something. "I'm going to think about it," she said. "I might speak to him. Or I might not. I really don't know."

Nineteen

June 1984

Please think of me

IT WAS SOME TIME before Julie went to see Mrs Donald. She had found it difficult to make up her mind, and it was over a week after her unsettling conversation with Angela that she had finally decided what she should do. It had not been an easy decision. Her surprise over James's behaviour had become resentment, and then finally anger. There were times when she had felt inclined to confront him, but she had not done so. She did not imagine that such a meeting would be at all easy. She would reveal her suspicions and remind him of the conditions of the lease – conditions that she had made clear to him right at the beginning. She would reproach him for putting her in a position in which she was in breach of her explicit undertaking to Mrs Donald. She would explain the lease might be cancelled if the lawyers found out they were in breach of one of the terms, and that his selfishness would in this way make five others homeless and scrabbling around to find a room in another flat. "It's not just about you, James," she would say.

She considered what his reaction might be. It was possible, she thought, that he would accuse her, no doubt, of being a prude – of accepting an unjustified curb on the freedom of action of a group of people who were adults, and capable of making up their own minds about their private lives. He would affect indignation that she should even speak to him about a policy that was clearly so old-fashioned as to be absurd. He would probably argue that there was no moral obligation to observe a pointless or restrictive provision that served no real purpose. They were careful tenants, he might say, and that was all that mattered.

Eventually she would speak to Mrs Donald. She would tell her what had happened and discuss with her what to do. It was likely, she felt, that the advice she would receive would be to raise the matter with James and to ask him to tell Lizzie to go. It was possible that Mrs Donald might herself have a word with Lizzie – she was, after all, one of her employers and could use the authority that conferred. It would be easier, Julie thought, for an older person such as Mrs Donald to step in and sort things out rather than to expect one of the flatmates themselves to do it. But that, she decided, would be unlikely to happen. This was her problem, and she could not dodge it. If, as she suspected, Mrs Donald would want Lizzie out, then she would pass on that message to James and insist on Lizzie's departure. Nobody could blame her for that, and she herself would not have the niggling worry that she had acted only because she somehow resented Lizzie's closeness to James.

When Julie appeared at the house, Mrs Donald gave her a warm welcome.

"I've been hoping you'd come to see me again," she said. "There are times when I feel starved of intelligent conversation. I sit here and brood, you see. I imagine that the city is full of people having earnest debates about this and that, and here am I, sitting in suburbia, so to speak, and excluded from all that fascinating talk."

Julie explained that there was something she needed to talk about – something to do with the flat.

Mrs Donald sighed. "The hot water system? The cooker? The window in that room in the back?" She sighed again. "The roof? Please not the cupola!"

"No, nothing like that."

Mrs Donald looked pleased. "A personal problem then? Somebody not behaving? Somebody not paying their share of the bills?"

Julie shook her head. "No . . . well, yes, in a way."

Mrs Donald waited.

"You remember that you said there was a strict limit on the number of people in the flat? Six."

Mrs Donald hesitated. It seemed to Julie almost as if she was expecting this. "Yes, I did say that."

"I'm afraid that there have been seven," Julie said. "I'm not sure for how long – but possibly as long as a month or so."

Mrs Donald was impassive. She didn't seem unduly surprised.

"One of the boys let his girlfriend move in," Julie continued. "Unofficially, you see. And—"

Mrs Donald suddenly raised a hand. "You don't need to go on," she said.

Julie caught her breath. If this was going to be a summary judgement – the announcement of the cancellation of the lease – then Mrs Donald was being calm about it.

"No?"

"No," said Mrs Donald. "I know all about this."

Julie stared at her in astonishment.

"You see," said Mrs Donald. "I played a part in bringing those two together. I know one should be careful about playing the matchmaker – you can get it all wrong."

Julie was struggling. "Do you mean –"

Mrs Donald interrupted her. "I made a bad mistake once," she continued. "We were invited to a cocktail party – I normally can't stand that sort of thing – but in this case we knew quite a few of the guests and it wasn't too much of an ordeal. One of them was a musician. He was a very talented trombone player. He freelanced for a lot of important orchestras. You heard him on the radio – on the jazz programmes. We ended up asking him to dinner, and he accepted.

"We then had to get a couple of other guests to make a party – and that's where we made our mistake. We both thought that we knew somebody who would get on well with him – a friend, Jane, who had been divorced a couple of years before, was roughly the same age as him, and was lively and attractive. She had mentioned to me that she wouldn't mind meeting somebody, and so I thought of her now. She enjoyed music, and they both lived in Edinburgh. I was aware that he was single, as he occasionally worked with another musician I knew, and she had mentioned that she thought he might be a good catch for somebody.

"The dinner party took place. We seated him next to Jane. His name was Martin. Very good-looking. Charming. And she was extremely attractive. Beautiful auburn hair. Lovely skin."

Mrs Donald paused. "You can tell that this is going to end badly?"

"I think I've worked that out," said Julie. "Disaster?"

Mrs Donald gave a rueful smile. "I'm afraid so. They got on famously at the dinner table – we almost had to call the fire brigade. Then I heard from her that she was seeing him regularly, and so I chalked that up as a success. I was quite smug about it. Most people love it when an attempt at matchmaking seems to work. They feel that they've somehow increased the amount of happiness in the world – which is no doubt true often enough."

"But not always," said Julie.

"No, not always. And certainly not in this case."

Julie asked what went wrong.

"Him. He went wrong. He'd always been wrong. He was extremely controlling."

Julie winced. "That's—"

"Something one can't live with. She had to run away from him – I mean, change her address, the lot. She even thought of getting a court order to keep him from pursuing her."

"A nightmare."

Mrs Donald agreed. "The poor woman was quite traumatised. She recovered, of course, but it took time. She never blamed us, though. She said that she was an adult and made adult choices. She chose to go out with him – we didn't oblige her to do that."

"But you still felt bad about it?" asked Julie.

"Massively. And you'd think I'd learned my lesson. But . . ."

Julie allowed herself a smile. "You succumbed to the temptation to play Cupid once more?"

Mrs Donald gave Julie an apologetic look. "I'm afraid so. I am so fond of Lizzie, you see. I wanted her to see something of a slightly wider world than that hotel kitchen of hers. I wanted her to meet somebody a cut above those ill-tempered chefs and so on. She's a lovely girl, you see, and I thought she deserved better."

Julie did not say anything. She began to see where this was leading, and she was astonished. Could Mrs Donald be about to say what she was beginning to suspect she might?

Mrs Donald read Julie's look correctly. "Yes," she said, lowering her eyes. "Yes. I deliberately brought Lizzie and James together."

She waited for a response, but before Julie could say anything, she went on. "I didn't have to do much. I simply introduced them – and let nature take its course. They took to one another immediately." She paused. "Does any of this surprise you?"

Julie thought for a few moments. Then she replied that if there was any surprise, it was over the fact that Mrs Donald should have tried to matchmake. "I'm not surprised that the two of them got on well together," she said. "James is a very nice guy. I don't know Lizzie really – but I can see the two of them getting on together just fine."

"Yes, they did," said Mrs Donald. "And then James came to see me and told me that he wanted Lizzie to live with him. He told me that he knew the lease allowed only six people to live in the flat. He asked me whether I would allow Lizzie to move in. In fact, he said she already had – but he wanted my approval. He said that he would feel bad about it otherwise. Naturally, I said that it was all right with me."

Julie frowned. If Mrs Donald had waived the restriction on numbers, then why had James bothered to conceal Lizzie's presence? Now she asked her this.

"I gather that she didn't want you and your friends to know," she said. "Apparently Lizzie felt a bit overwhelmed by the rest of you. There you were, highly educated, confident, able to express yourself effortlessly, and with style. She felt out of her depth." She paused. "I know it may be difficult to understand, but I think she would feel that she was somehow intruding on you."

Lizzie shook her head in incomprehension. "Why should she feel that?"

"Because it's only natural," said Mrs Donald. "If you haven't had much of an education, you can go through life regretting it. You might always feel at a disadvantage when you encounter people who have had what you haven't had. You just do. And for some people that can mean they don't have much confidence. You may not be able to do much about it. You don't necessarily get a second chance."

Julie nodded, but still she wanted to get one thing clear. "So you've known all along? You knew?"

"I did," said Mrs Donald. "I knew exactly what was happening. Does that surprise you?"

The question hung in the air between them. Julie was uncertain what she should feel. Surprise? Disappointment? Affront? Mrs Donald seemed to pick up on this uncertainty, as she reached forward and put a reassuring hand on Julie's arm. "I understand that you might feel a bit confused over this," she said. "It is a rather odd state of affairs, but I hope you can see it from my point of view. I really do want the best for that young woman. I've become very fond of her, you know – ever since she started to work for me." She gave Julie a searching look. "James is so *right* for her. I hope you can see that. He's so much better for her than those people she works with." She paused. "I know it sounds old-fashioned, but, in a way, James is her way out, if you see what I mean. He's her chance of something better."

Julie swallowed. What difference, she asked herself, does it make to me? None. But at the same time, what was she being asked to do, implicitly or otherwise?

The answer was not long in coming.

"Do you think you could pretend not to know?" asked Mrs Donald. "Do you think you could leave things as they are? Not notice that—"

"That somebody else is living in the flat?" Julie supplied.

Mrs Donald smiled. "I know it sounds a little much when put that way. But, yes."

Julie looked away. She would have to agree, she suspected, but she felt that the whole situation was absurd. Why should she make a pretence of not knowing about something that she did know about – purely to protect Lizzie's rather unnecessary feelings? If Lizzie felt awkward about living with them, then she could go and live somewhere else. Lizzie was not her problem.

Mrs Donald cleared her throat. "Of course, if you were to help us . . ."

Us? Julie wondered.

"If you were to make things easy for Lizzie in this way, then I would be only too happy to reduce the rent. As a gesture, you see."

Julie shook her head. That, she decided immediately, would complicate matters even further. She would be beholden to Mrs Donald, who would effectively be buying her charity. If helping Lizzie was the right thing to do – as Mrs Donald suggested – then she would not need to be bribed to do it.

She rose to leave. "It's all right," she said. "Things can go on as they are."

"You're very kind. And, you know, I think you're doing a very kind thing."

Julie hesitated. "Am I?"

"Yes," said Mrs Donald. "Sometimes people do kind things without realising that they are being kind. Perhaps that is what is happening here."

She left Mrs Donald's house and began to walk down Morningside Road, back towards the flat. It was early evening, and there were few people about on the street. This was the time when most people were already at home – tea time in Edinburgh – and before the night life of the city began. She passed a young man sitting on the pavement beside the door of a small grocery store. He had a paper cup beside him and a sign that said *Please think of me*. A few coins had been tossed into the cup and left there – an invitation to passers-by, a nudge to any charitable impulse they might feel.

Please think of me. It was what we all so often wanted to say, even if we did not always put it that way. But that was how it should be put, perhaps, because that lay at the heart of what we wanted from the world. It was a direct moral appeal.

She would, Julie thought. She would think of Lizzie, whom she hardly knew, and of James, whom she knew a bit better. She would think of Mrs Donald whom she suddenly saw for what she was – a woman motivated by kindness – a woman out of her time, a sort of throwback to an age when people did things for others in a rather paternalistic way, because they felt they knew what was best. The times were against such attitudes, but they were still there, in odd corners – and sometimes they worked, sometimes they helped. Edinburgh was an odd place: formalities persisted; one might still encounter elaborate politeness; one might still meet women like Mrs Donald: independent, intellectual, and completely sure of themselves, Jean Brodies who had survived the 1960s and the winds of modernity.

She would speak to Angela and explain the situation. She was sure that Angela would go along with what they were being asked to do. Angela was not selfish – anything but, and she had already said she did not want to do anything about the situation. And Georgia? There was no need to speak to her about it, as she did not believe that Georgia knew about Lizzie anyway. And nor did Neil and Ian – as far as she knew.

She looked up at the evening sky. It was that that faint blue so typical of northern skies: high, cold, indifferent to our little dramas below. She smiled. She was conscious of feeling happy, perhaps because a worrying issue had been unexpectedly resolved, or perhaps because the last of the daylight was gentle on the stonework of the buildings; warm gold, forgiving.

Twenty

June 1984

These things shouldn't matter

OVER THE TWO WEEKS that followed, Julie saw little of James, or indeed of any of her flatmates. She had a dissertation to complete, as did Angela, and both were finding the process demanding. Georgia, seemingly untroubled by academic commitments, was preoccupied with a charity run for which she was training, and Neil spent a few days in Orkney, where his parents were celebrating their thirtieth wedding anniversary. Ian was busy with coursework assignments, although when Julie saw him in the kitchen, he seemed relaxed and ready to chat. He cooked a meal for her on one occasion, and she reciprocated – more than once. At one of those meals, they talked until after eleven, discussing books they had read, films they liked, friendships, plans. Ian was hoping to go later that summer to Romania and then on to Greece. He had been reading Patrick Leigh Fermor and his imagination had been fired by the landscape portrayed in the account of that great walk. One day, he thought, he would like to do that – to stroll off, and keep walking into an unhurried limestone landscape; to drink young wine made on remote farms, and eat goat's cheese and chunks of bread under an echoing sky; all with the screech of cicadas in the background, and with no return date in mind. He would be on his own, in his imagination as in reality, but he was fairly accustomed to that.

The miners' strike ground on. In the papers and on television the images proliferated as tempers shortened. At pitheads, violent confrontations became more common as men on strike faced lines of police sheltering behind their shields like Roman legionaries. Anger infected the air, and always, in the background were scenes of quiet despair as the state asserted its authority over those who sensed that this time they might lose. These were the last efforts of an old working class, brought up in the embrace of small mining towns that had a pit at their heart. Hardship and suffering over the years had forged firm bonds, had created a unity of feeling that was bone-deep, and expressed in the banners, worked lovingly by the women, that they carried at their annual galas. At the pithead, the miners scrubbed each other's backs in the communal baths when they came up, covered in coal dust. They stood beside one another in the pubs. They knew the names of wives, children, parents. On the far side of these events was a world that had no place for these working traditions; a world that was much wider in its ambitions; a world where things would be made elsewhere; where quite different skills would be valued.

Angela's resentment grew. Going home, she saw the effect of the strike on people with whom she had grown up. People did not see that in Edinburgh, she felt. There were sympathetic voices, but most people did not feel the effects of what was taking place just a few miles away. It was as if Edinburgh were in a different country, she said. Georgia listened, and said yes, it was like that. But she was losing interest, and although she was still sympathetic to the miners, her views were beginning to change. It was not the simple matter she had thought it was. It could not go on for ever, and eventually people would have to see that compromise was inevitable. What was happening was sad, and it was brutal, but new industries would make up for it, she thought. You can't do the things you've always done when they become outmoded or unprofitable. What was the point? People could learn to do different things. But she did not express these views, least of all to Angela.

Julie told Angela about Mrs Donald's disclosure. "She came out with it, just like that," she said. "She knew. And she'd set the whole thing up in the first place."

Angela shook her head in disbelief. "Stupid old cow," she said.

"No," said Julie. "I don't think she is. Romantic, yes; stupid, no. She's no fool."

"So, what now?" asked Angela.

Julie shrugged. "We let things go on as they are."

Angela wrinkled her nose. "But is she still here? I haven't seen anything."

"Neither have I. I hardly ever see James. I assume she slips in and out. They stay in his room. It's peculiar. I couldn't live like that."

"I think it's ridiculous," said Angela. "If she's officially allowed to be here, why the secrecy?"

"Apparently she's shy," said Julie. "She feels somewhat daunted by us."

Angela looked dubious. "I can understand she might find Georgia a bit . . . a bit off-putting, but us? Why would she have difficulties with me? I'm dead ordinary."

"And so am I," said Julie.

Angela grinned. "You wouldn't be dead ordinary where

I come from," she said. "You're East Lothian. That's very different from West Lothian."

"These things shouldn't matter," said Julie.

"But they do, I'm sorry to say. They matter more than you think."

Julie said that whatever lay behind Lizzie's reticence, it was a fact, and there was nothing they could do about it. "We all have a flatmate we don't really know – or even see," she said. "It's odd, but does it make any difference? Probably not."

Angela agreed. "We're happy as we are, aren't we?"

Julie wondered whether there was irony in her words, but Angela's reply sounded quite sincere.

"I'm so glad you invited me to live here," she went on. "I've been really happy in this flat. So, thank you."

"I'm glad," said Julie. "I think we've all been happy in our individual ways."

"And the boys?" asked Angela.

"Them too. Ian's a bit quiet, maybe even a bit sad, I suppose. But he told me that he loves living here – with us. He said that very specifically."

"And Neil?"

"The same," said Julie.

Angela hesitated. Then she said, "Do you think that Ian likes Neil?"

Julie was cautious. She had not told anybody of that morning when she had seen the two of them asleep in each other's arms – nor had she mentioned the conversation she had had about it with Neil. "I don't think so," she said. "They're friends, but that's it."

Angela looked away. "Would it matter if they were more than that? I mean, would it matter to you?"

Julie shook her head. "Not in the slightest. But they aren't."

"What about you?" asked Angela.

Julie frowned. "Me?"

"Do you mind my asking you something?"

Julie shrugged. "No. You can ask. It depends, though, on what you want to know."

Angela was direct. "Could you fancy Neil?" She paused. "I said *could you* rather than *do you*. It's two different things."

Julie considered this. The conversation was taking an intimate direction that she had not anticipated, but she found she wanted to continue it.

"I could fancy him," she said. "Look at him. Who couldn't?"

Angela raised an eyebrow. "Some people might not."

This was followed by a silence, broken at length by Julie, who said, "I think Neil is a free spirit right now. He'll find somebody, I suspect, but not just yet."

"I see," said Angela.

And then, quite unexpectedly, the moment came when Julie and James talked. It happened on a Friday evening when the others were out, and Julie thought she was alone. She was in the kitchen when James came in and began to make himself a cup of coffee.

She said, "I can't drink coffee at night – or rather, I *don't* drink it after six. It keeps me awake."

He ladled coffee into the cafetière. "I need it to keep me awake tonight. I've got a deadline for a paper I'm giving."

"At those long Tuesday seminars of yours?"

"Yes."

She looked at him and wondered how he felt about deceiving her. How could he? It did not matter that he had received

Mrs Donald's blessing – the wrong lay in the fact that he was hiding something from his own flatmates.

He noticed her stare. "Have I said something?"

She bit her lip – and made her decision. "Wouldn't it be better," she said, "if you were honest with us?"

He seemed to freeze. Slowly he turned round. "Honest?"

"Yes. About Lizzie."

He put down the spoon he had been holding. Coffee grounds spilled on the surface of the counter. "What about her?"

She threw caution to the winds. "She's living here, isn't she."

He did not answer her question directly, but he shook his head.

She said, "I don't know why you feel you need to deny it. You shouldn't do that to the people you live with."

With one hand he ineffectually swept up the scattered coffee grounds. "She did. She isn't here now. It's over, you see."

His response silenced her.

"Lizzie and I split up a week ago."

She opened her mouth to speak, but no words came.

James shrugged. "It is what it is – and it's over."

"But . . ."

She did not finish. James raised a hand. "You don't have to say anything." He sighed. "There's not much that anybody can say in these circumstances. Somebody tells you they've broken up with someone and you say that you're sorry to hear it – even when you may be really pleased. You may not like the other person, for instance. But you don't say that, do you? You say, 'I'm sorry,' and then you try to think of something else to say, but there usually isn't anything much you can say."

Julie nodded. "You're right. Although I suppose you can ask why. You can ask what happened – especially if you liked the other person. And I liked Lizzie – although I didn't really know her."

He gave her a quizzical look. "Did you have an opinion? You only met her once, I think."

"She struck me as being . . ." Julie tried to remember what she had thought of Lizzie. "Sparky? Yes, I suppose I thought she was sparky."

James considered this. "Yes, you could say that. She was great company. She was unlike anybody I've ever met before. She was her own person. But she . . ." The sentence was left unfinished.

Julie waited. "But she?"

"She felt inadequate."

Julie asked why. "She was attractive. Lively – as you've said. She was good at her job."

James hesitated. It seemed to Julie that he was finding it difficult to express what he felt. "You don't have to tell me if you don't want to," she said.

He brushed this aside. "No, there's no reason for me not to. She was ashamed, you see. She was ashamed that she wasn't very well-educated. That's the way she put it, as it happens. She said, 'I'm not well-educated,' and then she said, 'You people are.' And by *you people* she meant you and me, you know. And Georgia and Angela and the guys. All of us."

Julie looked dismayed. "But that's ridiculous."

"Not if you're Lizzie," said James. "I tried to persuade her. I did my best. You know we sat there in my room and talked about books. She got books from Mrs Donald. She got them from me. And she read them. Then we'd discuss them for hours. She asked me to teach her philosophy. She'd got hold of Bertrand Russell's *History of Western Philosophy*. She went through it from cover to cover. Nobody reads that these days, but she did."

Julie felt a pang of regret. If only she had been able to talk to Lizzie, she might have been able to help her to see things in better perspective. That poor girl, hiding away because she felt intimidated . . .

"And then," James went on, "she moved out. I came back and found a note on my bed. I went straight to the hotel and asked to see her. They got her from the kitchens. They weren't too pleased, but they fetched her. And she told me then that she had decided she would never fit in. She said that she shouldn't have tried to be part of our world when she didn't belong there. She said that she wanted to talk to me about it but she felt that I would simply persuade her to stay and she would be unable to stand up for herself. She said she was sorry, but it would be best for me to find someone else – somebody else who belonged to the world she was trying to be a part of."

Julie shook her head in amazement. "But people change. They move between worlds, anyway. They always have. You don't have to stick to where you are. You don't have to stay where you started."

"I told her that," said James. "I tried to get her to see that. But she had made up her mind, and I knew that once she did that she wouldn't budge. That's what she's like."

Julie sat down. "I'm so sorry," she said. "I didn't know about any of this."

"No, but that's what has happened. Sometimes you think you have people in your life, but you don't really have them. Do you know what I mean?"

Julie thought that she did.

"Sometimes you lose people," James continued. "Sometimes

it hurts a lot. Like now. It hurts now."

"I'm very sorry."

He drew in his breath. "I was responsible for her coming here. I'm sorry about that – I shouldn't have kept it from you. But I suppose I didn't see any harm in keeping it secret. I spoke to Mrs Donald, you see. I had her permission."

"I know that."

Julie found it hard to imagine how Lizzie could have been in awe of her – or the others. "Nobody in this flat looks down on anybody else," she said.

James said he knew that. "But once you think something, you know, it's hard to rid yourself of an idea. Lizzie thought she would never have what you have. She would never be part of a real student flat." He looked at her. "And I went along with it. I shouldn't have, but I did. I didn't know, of course, that you knew. I feel bad about it now."

They looked at one another. There was no reproach in Julie's expression.

"I didn't mind," she said. "I hoped you would be happy, the two of you, and now I'm sorry that you aren't."

"I'll get by," said James.

"Were you in love with her?" asked Julie.

It took him a while to answer. Then he said, "Yes, I was. And maybe I still am."

"We're all in love, I think," said Julie. "Everybody in this flat is in love, in one way or another." She said that so easily, almost without thinking, and without being sure that this was what she really meant; as we sometimes say things that are completely true without first convincing ourselves that they are true.

"That happens," said James. "But if we can't be in love at this stage in our lives, then when could we ever be in love?"

He looked at her, and then went on. "I wish I could stay here much longer. I wish that we didn't have to split up and go our separate ways. I wish that we could continue, just as we are now." He paused.

"But we can't," he said eventually. "We can't do that because we are only here to prepare ourselves for something out there. We still have to go out there. We still have to say goodbye to the university and our friends and head off for whatever it is we're going to be doing for the rest of our lives, year after year."

"The real world?"

James made a gesture of acceptance. "Yes, you could put it like that. And it's sometimes a hard world, and an unkind one. And the story doesn't always end in the way we want it to. Look what's happening out there right now. A rather different, crueller world is being hammered out."

She lowered her gaze. She asked where Lizzie was.

"She's living somewhere down in Leith." Leith was the port of Edinburgh; a place of ships, and bonded warehouses, and different, sea-faring memories. To move to Leith was to move worlds.

"You're not going to try to see her again?"

He shook his head. "She doesn't want that."

She said, "I'm so sorry about all this, James."

He was standing close to her. Now he reached out and took her hand, saying quietly, "I miss her. I miss her really badly."

"Of course you do. Of course."

She could see his appreciation as he continued, "But if you fall in love quickly – as we did – then it shouldn't take too long to fall out of love. At least, that's what I hope."

She gave his hand a squeeze. They were more than flatmates now; they were friends, which was what she had always hoped for, right from the beginning.

He smiled. "Dear Julie," he said.

He leaned forward and planted a kiss on her brow. She closed her eyes, hoping despite herself that there might be another kiss. But there was not. Unbidden, the words came to her mind, the words she had learned in singing lessons when she was twelve. *Ae fond kiss.* One fond kiss, that's all. *Ae fond kiss, and then we parted . . .*

Twenty-One

June 1988

Together again

WHEN GEORGIA SUGGESTED TO her fiancé, Anthony, that they should get married in Scotland, he needed little persuading. He had no family connections with Scotland, but for some time he had been making regular business trips to Edinburgh and had struck up a number of friendships there. Georgia herself had left Edinburgh when she graduated and was now working for a business consultancy firm in London. She did not particularly like her job – she called it her *high-octane occupation* – and was now looking for another. She wanted something with less pressure, where she would not be working with people who were quite so determined to demonstrate their ability to work absurdly long hours without falling asleep.

Neither of them wanted a big wedding. Anthony had a small list of friends and a coterie of close relatives. For her part, other than immediate family, Georgia wanted to have four or five friends from London, along with their partners. But then she particularly wanted to invite the flatmates with whom she had shared the Marchmont flat. "I really want them there," she said to Anthony. "We're going to get married in Edinburgh and those people are Edinburgh to me. We lived together for two years. That means a lot."

"Of course," said Anthony. "But don't expect me to invite the guys from Kennington." That was where his student flat had been, and it was a place of mixed memories.

"It was different for me," said Georgia. "We were friends at a time when . . . well, at a time when friendship was very important."

"Isn't it important now?" asked Anthony.

"Of course it is," she said. "It's just that somehow the friends you have at that stage of life are unlike those you make later on. You are at the start line. You're never in that particular place again."

He asked her about them, and she replied, "I find it hard to describe them. We were very different from each other, but it seemed to work. I suppose you might say that we loved one another."

"Really?"

"Yes."

"And then—"

"And then we all went our separate ways. I felt so sad about that. It was the end of something very important for me."

He asked whether she thought they would come.

"We'll see," she said. "One lives in New York. Others are here and there – mostly in Scotland. One's up in Orkney."

He looked at her. He realised that there were parts of her life that he knew nothing about. Perhaps it was always like that with the person you married: discoveries came later. "It means a lot to you, doesn't it?"

She nodded. It might be unsettling, perhaps, to see them again – but it was what she wanted.

"Who's in New York?" asked Anthony.

"James. He was a postgraduate. He was doing a master's degree in philosophy. He kept to himself a lot, but we all liked him."

"Do you think he might come? New York isn't exactly next door."

"He might," said Georgia. "I already wrote to tell him. He said that he'd try to juggle it with his diary. I had the impression he was keen to come, if the others would be there."

"And will they?"

"Ian, definitely. He's in Edinburgh, so it's no problem for him. There's Neil up in Orkney, but he gets down to Edinburgh regularly, so he'll probably make it. That leaves Julie, who's in Glasgow, and Angela – I've mentioned her to you – she lives just out of town. Armadale."

"And that's it?" asked Anthony. "Five flatmates, plus you – to make six. Nobody else?"

Georgia hesitated, but only for a brief moment. "That's it," she said.

Ian was able to put them up for the three days they would be in Edinburgh for the wedding. Georgia was staying with her parents in a hotel, and Neil had a cousin in the New Town who offered him his spare room. The others – James, Julie and Angela – were easily fitted into the large flat that Ian had in Circus Place. The flat belonged to an aunt who had moved to France and who was happy for him to live in it.

"It's almost the same," he said to Julie as he showed her to her room. "Except that it's on the other side of town."

"And are we almost the same?" asked Julie.

Ian smiled. "You don't look any different. You still look as nice as you did three years ago."

That was the last time he had seen her – the day of their graduation. They had been in the crowd of graduates outside the McEwan Hall, all begowned and surrounded by family. They had spoken briefly, intending to have a longer conversation, and then suddenly he had looked about and she seemed to have been swallowed up by the crowd.

"And you're exactly the same," she said. "I don't want anybody to change, you know. I know it's unrealistic, but I'd like us all to be twenty-one for ever."

"A lot of people are," said Ian, and he laughed. "A lot of people don't get much beyond eighteen – inside, that is."

She agreed, and asked why this should be so. Were we afraid to grow up? Before he could answer, she asked, "Is the past safer than the future?"

He smiled. "Remember how we used to talk about things like that in the flat? In the kitchen?"

She did remember. But it was a fading memory now. In due course, she suspected she would forget it altogether.

"The past's less uncertain," Ian went on. "I suppose you can at least say that about it. The future has surprises – the past doesn't."

"You sound exactly like you used to sound," she said.

He grinned. "Pretentious?"

"No, you were never that. I wouldn't have liked you if you had been pretentious."

He put on an expression of mock surprise. "You mean, you liked me?"

She entered into the spirit of the exchange. "It's amazing, but yes, I liked you."

He seemed serious now. "I liked you too. I liked you a lot."

A silence ensued.

Then he said, "I always thought you liked Neil more than you liked me, you know. That's what I thought."

She did not reply immediately. She went to the window and looked out. The trees in the garden at the centre of Circus Place were in full leaf; branches swaying slightly in the wind. It was inevitable, she thought, that things would come out at a reunion like this; that things would be said that had been unsaid before.

He waited until she looked at him, and then he held her gaze. It was almost as if he was going to press home an accusation, she thought. Of course, he was right to see a difference in her attitude towards Neil. It *was* different; of course it was. With him it was a friendship; with Neil the potential for something quite different gave it an edge. And there was something else – something that she had spoken to nobody about and would certainly not speak to Ian about.

But then he said, "Was there ever anything between you and Neil?"

She was momentarily taken aback by his question, and Ian sensed that. His apology came quickly. "I'm sorry. I shouldn't have asked."

She recovered her composure. "I don't mind."

She remembered her conversation with Neil after she had inadvertently seen them together. Neil had told her that nothing had happened – that they had simply spent the night in the same room, on the same bed, in companionship. But Ian had never said anything to her about it. It was possible that Neil had told him he had explained everything to her, but it was equally possible that he had not. That meant that Ian might still believe she thought there had been more to it.

Now she asked him. "And you and Neil? Was there ever

anything between the two of you?"

For a time, the question hung in the air between them. She saw its effect on Ian. He swallowed. She echoed what he had said. "I shouldn't have asked."

He answered her directly. "No. Nothing. Ever."

"I thought not," she said.

He was staring at her intently, as if trying to make sense of something. Then he said, "But you saw us."

She nodded. "I did. But Neil told me that you had simply spent the night together as friends – that was all. He said there was nothing else." She paused. "Didn't he tell you that he spoke to me about it?"

Ian shook his head. "No. I sort of assumed that you must have thought we were—"

"Lovers? No. I didn't think that."

He seemed relieved. "Neil and I didn't talk about that night. Never."

She was surprised. "Not once?"

"No. We pretended it hadn't happened."

She considered this. She thought it was sad that embarrassment should prevent people from talking about things that really needed to be talked about – that they should tiptoe around moments of emotion.

"Do you think he was ashamed?" she asked.

He sighed. "Perhaps. But I think he was more likely worried about how I would react. I think he was afraid that I would expect it to become a pattern – spending the night together."

"Is that what you would have wanted?"

Ian looked away. "I don't know. Possibly, but I respected the limits. I could see there was never going to be anything more between us. So I deliberately didn't entertain the possibility.

I had the memory of that one night of . . . of being together. You know, that was all it was. Just lying there with my friend. That's all I wanted." He paused. "Can you understand what that meant to me? It meant that for a brief few hours *we* were all that mattered. That there was the world outside, everybody else, the whole deal, and then there was us together, just us. I had him to myself. That's what friendship is, isn't it? To have the other person to yourself. I think friendship's private – I've always thought that."

She looked at him. She had rarely, if ever, had a conversation with another person that was quite as intimate as this. She wondered what it cost him to speak so frankly; it could not have been easy. You bared your soul and you gave away something of yourself: some small piece of the armour, in which we wrap ourselves. And then you were naked, with all the vulnerability of those who have no clothing to protect them from the gaze of others.

She said, "I know exactly how you feel. I really do."

He met her gaze. "Do you?"

"Yes."

She made up her mind. There were moments when reciprocation was a moral necessity. She had to tell him.

"I was a bit in love with Neil too."

He barely reacted, but she knew that her words had had an effect. There was a slight change in his expression. Surprise? Perhaps even envy? It was hard to tell. Then he asked, "Did he know that?"

She nodded. "I think so."

"But you never told him?"

She thought it was not something that you always told people. Many people went through life without ever telling anybody about that, assuming that the person they loved would guess, or know. Love did not have to be spelled out, she thought.

Now Ian said, "Were you lovers?"

She hesitated, but knew that she would have to answer him. "No. Not really." And then she corrected herself. "Almost."

He looked amused. "Almost means . . . Well, what does it mean to almost be lovers?"

"We shared a shower once. Just once."

Ian's eyes widened. "In the flat?"

She nodded. "He suggested it. I thought he was joking, but he wasn't."

Ian digested this. "And that was it?"

"Yes."

Ian continued to hold her gaze.

She turned away. "I have thought about it time and time again. It was innocent – well, innocent in a way – but I haven't been able to forget it. I really haven't."

He stepped forward and put his arms about her. "Julie," he whispered. Her shoulders felt bony. He stepped back. She smiled at him, acknowledging that the embrace was, perhaps, not right for that particular moment.

"I knew that it wasn't anything very much for him," Julie said. "I knew that whatever I felt about him wasn't reciprocated. I knew it was hopeless."

He inclined his head. "Yes. Quite." He wondered whether she knew the reason. "He has somebody up in Orkney. He always has. They've known one another since they were fourteen. It's always been there."

"I know."

He waited for her to explain.

"He told me," she began. "He said that she was the only girl he'd ever loved – or would ever love."

Ian said, "He told me that too."

"So we both knew where we stood."

He inclined his head in mute acknowledgment. He did not think there was much to add – except for one thing. "I feel better for having known him. He's such a good friend. He's kind. He made me laugh."

"Yes. Me too."

Now Ian asked, "What are we going to do when we see him? He's coming down tomorrow. He phoned to tell me."

"We try not to cry," said Julie.

Ian smiled. "Sometimes that can be hard."

Julie said, "You know something? I wish we could go back to 1984. I wish we could be together again, in that flat, living with one another."

"You miss it?" asked Ian.

"I miss it more than I can say."

"And I suppose I do, too," he said. Then he continued, "They said it would get better. They said that when we went out into the world and started to earn our living and bought somewhere to live and did all those things, they said it would get better. But I don't think it does. I still think of how it was then, and about how fortunate we were to have what we had. And I'm worried that I'll never again have the chance of friendships that are so important to me as the friendships I had then."

Julie felt that too. "No, maybe not," she said.

"And then I think: you can't live in the past. You have to get on with life and stop thinking about how happy you once were. You have to put it behind you. You might even have to make a conscious effort to forget it, because otherwise it will always be there, trying to get you back."

She was concerned that their conversation could become maudlin. She asked about Angela. Did Ian see her regularly? He did, he said. He saw her every few months. She came into town and they would meet for coffee or for lunch. Sometimes three or four months would go by without their seeing one another, but then he would get in touch and they would make an arrangement.

"Is she happy?" asked Julie.

"I think so. Yes, I think she is. Not deliriously happy, perhaps, but happy enough."

"She's in the same job?"

"Yes. She's with an adult literacy programme out there. I think she likes the work. Although . . ."

"Although?"

"She's says that the heart has been taken out of those mining villages. She says their spirit's broken."

"We saw that," said Julie. "We were there at the time. Remember? The miners' strike was the final act."

"Angela is doing her best," said Ian. "She wants to do whatever she can. The work she's in gives her that feeling."

Julie asked him if he knew whether Angela had anybody in her life. "I always thought that she might be one of those people who are better by themselves."

"There's a man," said Ian. "He's a teacher in the high school in Bathgate. He's divorced. He has a young child. I don't know much more about him."

"Angela is a good friend," said Julie. "I'd like to see more of her. Glasgow isn't all that far away, but sometimes it's as if we're on another planet."

"We'll see her later today."

"And James too?" she asked.

"He's arriving tomorrow," Ian said. "Then we'll all be together again."

"Yes," muttered Julie. "You might say that."

He did not hear what she said. It was probably unimportant, he thought.

The next day, Georgia was too busy with last-minute arrangements to be there, but the others were, seated round the table in Ian's flat. James had flown in that morning and had caught up on sleep during the afternoon, and Angela and Neil had arrived within a few minutes of one another. Now, as Ian brought out the first course of the meal he had prepared, Julie looked round the table and smiled.

"I never dreamed this would happen," she said. "And all that it took was for Georgia to get married."

James laughed. "She should do that more often. Then we could all meet regularly."

"Has anybody met him?" Angela asked.

"I met him once," said Julie. "We went for dinner at a restaurant in Leith."

"And?" asked Angela.

"He's all right," said Julie.

"Faint praise," Neil remarked.

Julie had not intended to sound lukewarm. "No, he's nice enough. I wouldn't necessarily go for him, but then I'm me and Georgia's Georgia."

"He's a money person," said Angela. "They're a bit . . ."

Julie shook her head. "No, he's not like that. He's quite

thoughtful, as far as I can make out. And Georgia likes him. So that's all that matters."

"She's going to be well-off," said Angela. "Mind you, she always was."

Neil gave her a warning look. "You shouldn't judge people by their background."

Angela looked chastened. "I wasn't judging anybody."

"I don't think we should argue," said Julie. "We haven't got all that much time."

"Before?" asked Ian.

"Before we say goodbye again," Julie replied. "A couple of days – that's all we have."

"Nobody has all that much time, period," said James.

Ian said he thought that was being a bit morbid. "We have to act as if we're around for quite a long time," he said. "Otherwise, we wouldn't do anything. We'd sit around passively."

"James is the philosopher," said Angela. "You shouldn't take his lines."

James laughed. "I was never very good at aphorisms. Mind you, neither was Immanuel Kant."

"But I thought he said *Do as you would be done by*," said Neil. "That sounds aphoristic to me."

"Something of a simplification, but close enough," said James.

Ian gave James a quizzical look. "Haven't you given up on philosophy, James? Aren't you running a speakers' bureau?"

James replied that that was what he did. "But any job has its philosophical implications. Everything has its moral challenges. I encounter them daily. I have to represent people I disagree with, for instance. What do I do? Get them bookings even if I disagree with everything they have to say?"

Julie remembered something. "What about that character you told us about? What was his name? The one who went round giving talks about how to marry money?"

James grinned. "Larry Buckle? I'm surprised you remembered him."

"How could I forget?" said Julie.

"He's retired," said James. "But his place has been taken – there are several people on our books who are vying for the position of tackiest speaker. We have a whole bunch of retired actors who were on shows that nobody remembers any more. One does a talk on dogs in Hollywood – dogs owned by stars. He gets booked a lot."

Julie asked about the dogs – was there a Hollywood type?

"They were all neurotic," James said. "One of the dogs he talked about was said to have committed suicide. He shows a picture of one of Marilyn Monroe's dogs – she had a few, including one called Grover that Frank Sinatra had given her. Anyway, apparently, it bit the President of the United States and was almost shot by the Secret Service. That sort of thing."

Ian and Angela started a conversation among themselves. Neil joined in. Julie reached out to touch James on his arm. He smiled at her. "So," he said. "Back together. It doesn't seem to be three years, does it?" He paused. "Are you doing okay?"

"Yes. I'm fine."

He asked her what she was doing, and she told him about the gallery job she had in Glasgow. "I'm not sure how to describe my job. I do all the things the boss doesn't want to do. I don't mind. I'm lucky to have a job in the arts."

James glanced across the table at Ian. "And Ian?" he asked.

"He's working in a deli," Julie said. "It's not a very big one. He knows the woman who owns it and she offered him a job. He said he never imagined that's where he'd end up, but he really likes it."

"I'd change places with him, any day," said James. There was ruefulness in his voice.

"You don't like what you're doing? The family business?"

"It's okay, I guess. It's just that it's not how I want to spend my time. When we were all students, remember how we thought we had all the time in the world. We thought we could do job after job until we found one we liked. Nothing was for ever. Then we discover that it is, and we realise we have to try to get it right."

"True. And so?"

"I'm going to get out of the bureau. A cousin of mine is working there too – he likes it. He can take it over."

"And you?" asked Julie.

"I'm going to come back here. I've been thinking of it for some time, and I've already done something about it."

Julie brightened. "Back to Scotland?"

James nodded. "I've still got most of the money I was left by my uncle. It's even grown, apparently. There were some shares in a waste disposal company in Cincinnati. They were taken over by some people in California and suddenly became more valuable. There's money in garbage. I could get by for six years if I didn't eat lunch every day."

Julie laughed. "And with lunch?"

James shrugged. "Five years, easily."

"But what are you going to do here? Aren't there visa issues, or something like that? Work permits and so on?"

"I'm going to do a PhD – I'm permitted to be a student here again. I know what I want to write about. It's an odd corner of philosophy that bubbles away in the background. The issue of continuity of identity. Are we the same person through time? Am I the same person as the ten-year-old me?"

Julie smiled. "Of course, you are. You're just older. And you don't need a PhD to understand that."

James came up with another example. "Or dementia. Is the person with dementia the person they were before the illness? Or somebody who undergoes a profound conversion. People like that talk about *the new me*, but is there really a new person there?"

"Of course not," said Julie. "They're the same person, but with new attitudes."

James raised an eyebrow. "But is personhood just a matter of the physical person? Or is it something more – a sense of self persisting over time?"

Julie shrugged.

"It's not simple," said James. "You should read the literature."

"There's a lot of it?"

"Volumes," said James. "And there'll be even more when I add to it with my PhD." He became serious. "I'm not the same person as I was when I first came to Edinburgh. I'm different. And you . . . I suspect you are too."

She was silent. Was she? She cast her mind back. And suddenly she thought of Georgia. "I think Georgia changed," she said, and added, her voice lowered, "Angela showed her something, I think. Remember the strike? The visits to Armadale? I think the scales fell from her eyes."

James glanced across the table. Angela was still deep in conversation with Ian and Neil. He turned to Julie. "Angela was the one who didn't change. Out of all of us, she was the most rooted."

"Yes," said Julie. She liked the word *rooted*. If you were rooted, you knew who you were, where you had come from, and what you had to do. She herself was not rooted, she thought; or if she was, her roots were not as deep as Angela's were.

Julie looked at him tenderly. "And what about Lizzie?"

James's face fell. "I'm so sorry about that. I didn't handle it very well."

Julie said that it was not his fault she had left him.

"I think it was," said James. "I think she was looking for a deeper commitment. I don't think I gave her that. I wasn't thinking in those terms at the time." He looked away. "I still think of her a lot, you know."

"She's living down in Leith still," said Julie. "I saw her, you know. It was about four or five months ago."

His voice dropped. "You saw Lizzie?"

"Yes. She's working in a restaurant down there. It's one of those well-known places. She came out of the kitchen to speak to somebody, and I saw her. She didn't see me, and she went back into the kitchen pretty quickly. I toyed with the idea of going and asking for her, but I decided not to."

For a while, James said nothing. Then he said, "Where is this place?"

She told him, adding, "Would you like to see her?"

Her question clearly unsettled him. He did not reply immediately, but then he said, "I doubt if she wants to see me."

She challenged this. "You can't say that. You could try. If she doesn't want to see you, she'll tell you." She did not tell him that Lizzie had looked worn and tired to her.

He looked doubtful. "Possibly. I'll think about it."

On the other side of the table, a burst of laughter reminded them that there was another conversation at the table.

"What's so amusing?" asked Julie.

Ian pointed at Neil. "Him."

"Everything's amusing," said Neil. "All this. Our being back together like a bunch of students."

"They're very immature, these two," said Angela, smiling. "I should talk to you and James instead. Adult company, you see."

Julie rose from the table to fill their depleted wine glasses. Ian raised his in a toast. "To us," he said.

Julie returned to her seat and picked up her glass. She felt happy and sad at the same time. The wedding was two days away. They would have dinner again tomorrow here in Ian's flat. She had offered to cook something. Life must be so hard, she thought, to dislike the job you do. Or what you were. Or the people you have to live with. The last of these was the most difficult, she felt.

Unbidden, the memory came to her of the lecture she had attended all those years ago, when they had looked at *Landscape with the Fall of Icarus*, and Dr Brock had recited those words by Auden about how suffering happened in the middle of what we were doing in our ordinary lives. And so we didn't notice it, but we get on with our business as if it weren't happening.

She turned to James. "Go and see her," she said, and there was urgency in her voice. "Tell her that we'd like to see her too."

"I don't think so."

She lowered her voice. "Listen, when I saw her, I thought that she did not look happy. Okay, it was only for a few minutes. But you can tell, you know. You really can."

Angela surveyed the table over the top of her wine glass. "To nobody in particular," she said, adding, "What would it be like if we were all to live together again?"

"Sad," said Neil.

Ian disagreed. "I don't think so. We could live here in this flat. There's plenty of room."

"I happen to work in Orkney," said Neil. "James works in New York. Julie does something in Glasgow." He caught Julie's eye, and smiled mischievously.

Ian shrugged. "Then just the rest of us."

James said, "I'd like that."

Julie turned to him. "Would you?"

"Yes. I'm serious. I think our Marchmont flat worked very well."

Neil shook his head. "You can't go back. You never can."

Later that evening, James found the restaurant that Julie had mentioned. He went there shortly after eleven, when the last customers were preparing to leave. A waitress looked at him in astonishment: who wandered into a restaurant at this hour? She said, "It's far too late, sorry. We're closing now."

But he simply asked, "Is Lizzie here, please? I need to speak to her."

She emerged from the kitchen, wiping her hands on a piece of blue kitchen roll. When she saw him, she stopped in her tracks. He walked towards her, smiling, and said, "Yes, it's me." Then he said, "Lizzie, Lizzie, Lizzie."

She reached for a chair. He steadied her; he thought she was going to collapse: it would not have surprised him had she done so. He sat down beside her. One of the departing guests glanced at them as if she had sensed the momentous nature of the encounter. She nudged a fellow guest, and mouthed something: perhaps *Big emotional scene alert* . . . James did not care. He took Lizzie's hand in his. It seemed so warm. He stroked it gently. She looked down at the floor, as if she did not dare look at him. He said, "Julie told me you were here."

Then he said, "I only want to talk to you if you are happy to talk to me. Perhaps you don't want to. Just tell me – all right?" He paused. "If you can't . . . If you can't because you're with somebody else and, well, you just can't, I'll go away. But if you can, please let me talk to you."

She hesitated, and he thought she was going to say no. He thought: *my world depends on this moment*. But her hesitation was only to find the words. At length she said, "I'd like to talk to you."

He said, "Good." And then he said, "Could you take tomorrow night off?" He nodded in the direction of the kitchen. "From this place?"

She answered immediately. "Yes. I just don't turn up."

"No," he said. "Tell them."

She frowned. "What? Tell them what?"

He squeezed her hand. "Tell them you have an engagement party."

They sat at the table in Ian's flat. Even after nine, evening sun bathed the stone of the windows with gold. Julie looked at Lizzie, who was seated one place away, with Ian on one side and James on another. Julie thought that she looked young to be a mother of a three-year-old child; or was it a four-year old? There were circumstances in which the timing could be important; they were now. She glanced at James. He was smiling as he looked up at the ceiling. There was nothing there, but a small line of light, reflected from the window. Gold. Shimmering. Impermanent. Fatherhood. She thought she might say to him, "Fatherhood becomes you."

And love, she thought, becomes us all. Along with friendship. *Agape*, that disinterested love of others that we may all discover, in our different ways, if we are fortunate enough.

What would it be like to live together again? She savoured the thought.

She noticed that Ian was looking at her from over the table, smiling. She blew him a kiss. He blew it back.

A NOTE ON THE AUTHOR

SIR ALEXANDER McCALL SMITH is one of the world's favourite authors, with more than a hundred books to his name. These include novels in the award-winning and highly successful series *The No. 1 Ladies' Detective Agency*, which has sold over twenty million copies, and *44 Scotland Street* – the world's longest-running serial novel. He lives in Edinburgh, devotes his time to the writing of fiction, poetry and libretti, and has seen his books translated into over forty-six languages.

'A treasure of a writer whose books deserve
immediate devouring'
Guardian

'Perfect escapist fiction'
The Times

'One of the most entrancing treats of many a year'
The Wall Street Journal

'It's hard to find fault with such good-natured and
pleasurable optimism'
Observer

'I can think of no author writing today so deserving
of an enormous audience'
New Statesman

'A joyous, charming portrait of city life and human foibles,
which moves beyond its setting to deal with deep moral
issues and love, desire and friendship'
Sunday Express

'A new adventure in a series that
shows no signs of dropping in popularity or standard'
Daily Telegraph

'A charming, entertaining and uplifting book'
Daily Express